TWO GU...

Jake Warren, owner of the Diamond D ranch near Santa Rosa, New Mexico, desires to add the Lazy A spre... ... his property and to run the to... ... Two men stand in his way, Mal C'... ...ents, property owner in Santa Rosa, ...nd the sheriff, Frank McCoy. Warren frames McCoy for the murder of Mal Clements, but McCoy escapes from jail with the help of his girl, Abbe Clements, who believes in his innocence, and of his deputy, Mark Stevens. They have already sent word about the trouble to Frank's brother Dan, sheriff of Red Springs – can he clear his brother's name?

TWO GUN JUSTICE

TWO GUN JUSTICE

by

Jim Bowden

Dales Large Print Books
Long Preston, North Yorkshire,
BD23 4ND, England.

British Library Cataloguing in Publication Data.

Bowden, Jim
    Two gun justice.

    A catalogue record of this book is
    available from the British Library

    ISBN   978-1-84262-641-2 pbk

First published in Great Britain in 1961 by Robert Hale Limited

Copyright © Jim Bowden 1961

Cover illustration © Gordon Crabb by arrangement with
Alison Eldred

The moral right of the author has been asserted

Published in Large Print 2009 by arrangement with
Mr W. D. Spence

Dales Large Print is an imprint of Library Magna Books Ltd.

Printed and bound in Great Britain by
T.J. (International) Ltd., Cornwall, PL28 8RW

Chapter One

'The answer is no, McCoy, and always will be so long as you wear that star!' The small, fat man immaculately dressed in three-quarter length, black coat, fawn trousers and fancy waistcoat sat down behind the huge, oak desk and picked up a pen as if to write finish to the interview which had just taken place.

'But, Mr Clements...' The slim, fair-haired cowboy with a star pinned to his checked shirt started to protest. His youthful blue eyes flashed angrily.

'It's no use,' interrupted Clements. 'You and Abbe have known my views for some time now. If you'd thought anything about them you'd have done something or stopped seeing each other.' He rubbed his black moustache and looked down at the papers in front of him.

Anger flowed in Frank McCoy's face. 'You know how Abbe an' I feel towards each other. She doesn't mind marryin' a sheriff.'

'Look here, McCoy,' snapped Clements,

irritated that the young man should pursue the matter, 'I don't object to you personally. But Abbe's not marrying a lawman. I'm thinking only of Abbe; she can be a widow any day so long as you wear that star. If only you'd give it up; get a ranch and turn to cattle raising.'

'I'm a sheriff,' replied McCoy. 'Put in by the people of Santa Rosa as you well know. I'd be failing them if I didn't stick to my job.'

'You'll have to give it up if you want my daughter,' snorted Clements, now thoroughly angered by McCoy's stubbornness.

'An' be branded a coward!' shouted Frank leaning over the desk and glaring at the fat, prosperous saloon owner who leaned back in his swivel chair. 'You know full well what people would say if I threw in the job now. There's trouble comin' to Santa Rosa in the shape of Jake Warren an' the towns-folk would say I got out to save my hide.'

'You exaggerate their feelings,' snapped back Clements.

'Abbe wouldn't want me to turn in my star,' stormed McCoy. 'She wouldn't want to be married to a man who'd be known as "Runner" McCoy for the rest of his life.' He turned away in disgust snatching his brown

Stetson from the desk. Suddenly he swung round and spoke with great deliberation. 'Get this straight, Mister Clements, I'll figure some way. There's nothin' more certain that Abbe and I will marry.'

Frank flung open the door angrily and almost collided with a tall, dark, broad-shouldered cowboy who stood grinning in his path. He was immaculately dressed in a black shirt topping black trousers neatly folded into the top of black riding boots. His black, wide-brimmed sombrero was set at an angle to command attention and revealed thick black hair coming down in side-winders to the angle of his jaw.

'Howdy, sheriff,' he greeted. 'Havin' words?'

'Snoopin' Warren?' snapped Frank.

Jake Warren strolled passed the sheriff into the room. 'Mornin' Clements,' he said. 'People shouldn't raise their voices in argument if they don't want to be heard outside.' He grinned from one to the other.

Frank glanced sharply at Clements before turning to Warren. His eyes narrowed. 'I guess you could stoop as low as blackmail,' he said between tight lips. 'But I'm warnin' you now, Warren, keep clear of the law.'

Before the black clothed cowboy could

reply Frank swung round and left Clements' room. As the door closed behind the sheriff Warren turned to the saloon owner, a grin splitting his face.

'Wal, our sheriff seems to be in a bad mood this mornin', but from what I heard I don't blame him.' Warren sat down in the chair on the opposite side of the desk to Clements. He leaned forward without a word and helped himself to a cheroot from the box on the desk. He lit it slowly, watching Clements through the curling smoke. When the cheroot was lit to his satisfaction he leaned back in the chair and tipped his Stetson to the back of his head.

'Aren't you speakin' this mornin', Clements?' he asked.

'I'll say the same to you as I said to McCoy,' said Clements angrily. 'The answer is still no and always will be.'

'But what I offer you is a small fortune,' replied Warren smoothly.

'It is, but I aren't selling the Ace of Spades nor any of my property,' replied Clements. 'Now get out of here, I'm busy and I'd be mighty obliged if you didn't trouble me again.'

The grin left Jake Warren's face. He leaned forward crashing his fist on the desk. 'Your askin' fer trouble,' he snarled.

Clements rose slowly to his feet. 'If it's trouble you want, Warren, you can have it.' He flicked his coat to one side and patted the Colt holstered on his right thigh. 'I'm mighty useful with this, mighty useful.' He leaned forward across the desk glaring at the cowboy. 'I wouldn't sell you anything to let you get a hold in this town,' he hissed, 'least of all the Ace of Spades which you'd turn crooked as soon as you got it. I pride myself that things have kept the right side of the law here and I aim to keep them that way. You stick to your ranching, Warren. Now I'd be obliged if you'd leave.'

Jake Warren rose slowly to his feet; his face dark with anger at this rebuff. He faced Clements coldly across the desk, took a long draw at his cheroot and blew a cloud of smoke into Clements' face. The saloon owner clenched his fists tightly. His knuckles stood out white as he fought to keep his temper. His face reddened but he did not speak.

'I'll say the same as McCoy,' said Warren, his voice quiet but full of meaning. 'I aim to get what I want; I'll figure some way. That makes two of us, Clements, so you'd better watch your step.'

Warrant turned from the desk and hurried

11

from the room. Clements watched him go, cold hate in his eyes. As the door closed he slumped into his chair breathing deeply.

Warren hurried along the passage, angry at the continued frustration of his plans. One man prevented him from ruling Santa Rosa and the surrounding countryside and that man was Mal Clements. Clements owned all the important sites in the town and the immediate countryside so that any future development in Santa Rosa would be in his favour and Warren knew that a boom would come. If he was to reveal just one piece of information known only to himself Mal Clements would be a much richer man but if he could persuade Clements to sell–!

Warren reached the end of the passage and entered the huge, gaudily decorated saloon. It was quiet at this time of the morning. Four cowboys leaned against the long shining bar, five more occupied a table playing poker. The rest of the room was deserted except for two white- aproned barmen who swept the floor.

Jake Warren paused as he entered the saloon. His eyes moved slowly round the room, across the deserted stage, along the silent balconies which were crowded every night, and on to the still gambling tables which brought Mal Clements a fortune.

Warren sauntered over to the bar and ordered a drink. As he sipped his whisky he saw the room through half closed eyes and he could see himself strolling through a crowd greeting his customers who poured money into his pockets.

Suddenly he was startled back to reality by the harsh laugh of one of the poker players. Angrily he threw down the remains of his cheroot and ground it into the floor with his heel. He finished his drink with one gulp and as he put down the glass he glanced at the two cowboys who leaned against the counter. He nodded almost imperceptibly to them and when he saw them acknowledge his signal he turned towards the door. He was half way across the room when he was stopped by angry voices. He swung round in time to see the two men lean across the counter, grab the bartender and haul him over the bar. They each seized an arm and a leg and with one swing threw the man back over the counter to hit the huge mirror on the wall. With an ear-splitting crack the glass shattered and as the man crashed to the floor bottles and glasses which lined the shelves beneath the mirror were smashed to destruction.

The two cowboys roared with laughter as

they leaned across the counter. 'Thet'll teach you not to insult men from Missouri by tryin' to cheat them,' drawled one of the roughnecks.

Suddenly their laughter was halted by a quiet but authoritative voice. 'That will be a hundred dollars after you've apologised to my man.'

The two cowboys turned slowly to find themselves staring into the cold Colt held by Mal Clements who had hurried to the saloon on hearing the crash of the shattering mirror. They stared incredulously at the small, immaculately dressed saloon owner.

'But we ain't got a hundred dollars,' protested one of the roughnecks.

Jake Warren, who had silently watched the events, smiled to himself, moved slowly forward and leaned on a table close to Clements.

'That's too bad,' hissed Mal. 'Joe,' he called to one of the sweepers, 'get the sheriff.'

The man addressed as Joe dropped his brush without a word and ran from the saloon. A moment later McCoy hurried through the open door taking in the whole situation with one quick glance.

'What's the trouble, Clements?' he asked sharply.

'These two hombres cut up rough and now refuse to pay for the damage,' replied the saloon owner.

Frank faced the two cowboys but did not recognise them. His searching eyes saw two men in their early thirties; their battered sombreros matched their worn clothes and smooth-butted Colts hung low in their holsters. The sharp hawk-like features of one was in marked contrast to the round full face of the stouter cowboy.

'Who are you?' asked Frank..

'Couple of drifters,' replied the thin man casually. 'Jest passin' through.'

'The barman tried to cheat us with our change so we taught him a lesson,' explained the stout cowboy.

'Reckon you were mistaken,' retorted Clements icily. 'Dave wouldn't try anything like that.' His voice was quiet but full of determination. 'Pay for the damage right now.'

The man with the hooked nose grinned. 'I figure you've got a nerve,' he drawled. 'We come...'

'You'd better pay for the damage,' cut in Frank sharply.

The cowboy's eyes narrowed as he stared at the sheriff. 'We ain't payin' cos we can't.'

'Then, I figure you'd better have a look at our jail,' replied Frank. He watched the two men closely as he saw them tense themselves but before the situation could explode a voice spoke behind him.

'I reckon I can settle this matter, McCoy.'

Frank turned to see Jake Warren pulling a roll of money from his pocket. 'I think I heard you say a hundred dollars, Clements. Will that do?' Warren threw ten ten dollar bills on to a table.

Clements slowly holstered his gun. 'Reckon so,' he muttered eyeing Warren suspiciously.

'Satisfied, McCoy?' asked Warren smoothly, a glint of satisfaction in his eyes.

Frank nodded and moved across to Clements as he picked up the money.

'Wal, thet's mighty generous of you, stranger,' acknowledged the thin-faced cowboy. 'The least we can do is to buy you a drink.'

'Not fer me, thanks all the same,' replied Jake. 'I reckon you'd better keep your money if you're short.'

'Guess we should at that,' laughed the cowboy. He turned to his companion. 'C'm on, Clay, I reckon we'll mosey along.'

Without a further word the two men left the saloon. As they passed out on to the sidewalk a cowboy who had watched the

16

incident from further along the bar hurried to Frank.'

'Know who those two are?' he asked, a note of excitement in his voice.

Frank looked curiously at the man. 'No,' he replied crisply.

'Thought I'd seen them somewhere when they came in but it was only when I heard the name Clay that I realised who they were.'

'Wal,' said Frank as the excited cowboy paused for breath, 'who are they?'

'Ever heard of the Harper bunch?'

Frank was startled. 'Sure,' he said. 'Bunch of robbers an' killers that terrorised Southern Missouri.'

The cowboy nodded excitedly. 'Yeah, that's right. I was in Missouri way back; heard a lot about the Harper bunch; saw them several times. When Red Harper was gunned down the gang split up. Those two hombres rode with Harper; Clay Duncan an' Ed Mason.'

'You sure?' asked Frank.

'Never more certain,' came the reply. 'Two of the best gunmen Harper had. Mighty good job you had your Colt in your hand when you came in, Mr Clements.'

Frank looked curiously at Jake Warren. 'You were ready to help them; did you know

17

who they were?' he asked.

Jake shook his head. 'Never seen 'em before.'

'Why did you pay Clements?' snapped Frank.

Warren grinned. 'Don't want any of my potential customers to git a bad impression,' he replied smoothly as he turned on his heel and left the saloon.

Frank, a thoughtful expression on his face, watched him go. 'I wonder,' he said half to himself.

'So I do,' commented Clements.

'What are you thinkin'?' asked Frank curiously.

'It could have been a put up job to warn me what will happen if I don't sell out to Warren. If he's brought in hired guns then he means business!'

Chapter Two

When Frank left the Ace of Spades he paused on the sidewalk. He glanced along the street and noticed Jake Warren crossing the dusty road towards the Bank. In the opposite direction the two gun-slingers were already riding out of town at a steady trot.

Frank rubbed his chin thoughtfully as he watched them go. Suddenly, as if he had come to some decision, he hurried across the street, unhitched his horse from the rail outside his office and swung into the saddle. He turned the black, powerful horse and followed them.

A quarter of a mile from Santa Rosa the two riders swung east and put their horses into a steady gallop. The country was undulating and Frank had no difficulty in keeping the men in sight whilst keeping well back along the trail. The trail they were riding was taking them further from Warren's spread and when, after crossing a wide stream, they put their horses into a fast gallop Frank drew rein and decided that his hunch that they would return to town or Warren's ranch was wrong. He watched them ride out of sight before turning his horse and retracing his steps even more puzzled by the fact that Warren had paid for the damage in the saloon.

When he reached the outskirts of Santa Rosa Frank turned from the trail and headed for a house which stood on a slight rise a short distance away. As he swung from the saddle beside the white railings a dark-haired girl rose from a chair on the verandah and hurried to meet him. Frank watched her with admiration. Her slim figure was accentuated by the tight-waisted, brightly-coloured, gingham frock. She smiled happily showing a row of white, even teeth; her brown eyes sparkled and her hair, which fell around her shoulders, framed a rounded face.

Frank took her hands and kissed her lightly before walking slowly towards the verandah.

'Sorry I'm late,' apologised Frank. 'Couple of gun-slingers I had to watch. Seems they've left town.'

Abigail looked eagerly at Frank. 'What did daddy say?' she asked.

Frank frowned and shook his head as they sat down on the verandah steps. 'No use,' he murmured. 'His answer was the same. He doesn't want you to marry a lawman.'

The girl's face clouded, she looked anxiously at Frank who stared at his sombrero as he casually flicked dust from it. Suddenly, he looked up and stared deep into Abbe's brown eyes as if searching for something.

'Abbe,' he whispered, 'do you want me to hand in my badge?'

The girl matched Frank's look as she took hold of his hand. 'I love you, Frank, and I live in dread and fear of hearing that you've been gunned down, but I know how you feel about the job and I wouldn't want to live the rest of my life with a man who always thought he'd run out on a job.'

Frank smiled his thanks and leaned forward to kiss Abbe.

'We must be patient a little longer, darling,' the girl continued. 'You do see, don't you, that I don't want to go against daddy's wishes at the moment especially with mother just dead a year. Don't worry, I know something will turn up very soon and everything will be all right.'

Frank's eyes narrowed and when he spoke his voice was full of determination. 'It certainly will; I'll see it is.' Suddenly he changed the subject. 'Your father won't sell out to Jake Warren will he?'

Abbe stared at Frank in surprise. 'No, I don't think so,' she replied quietly. 'He doesn't like Warren and doesn't want to see his sort running Santa Rosa. Why do you ask?'

'I'm afraid there might be trouble,' answered Frank and went on to relate what had happened in the Ace of Spades. 'I'm almost glad things are coming to a head. When this job is settled, Abbe, I'll retire and become a cattleman.'

About an hour later Frank left Abbe and after attending to two jobs outside of town he returned to Santa Rosa. He turned his horse in at the livery stable and after a brief visit to his office he headed for the room he rented at the hotel. Light was fading from the sky and as he walked along the sidewalk the busy and noisy night life of Santa Rosa was beginning.

He entered the hotel, nodded to the clerk behind the desk and went straight upstairs eager to get the dust of his ride washed off. All was quiet along the corridor as he opened the door to his room. He stepped inside and froze in his steps. The faint light revealed a huddled figure sprawled on the floor. The curtains flapped gently in the breeze against the open window which overlooked the balcony. Frank knew he had left the window shut when he had left that morning. A dull thud as if someone had dropped from the balcony galvanised the sheriff into action. He crossed the room in three quick strides, drawing his Colt as he did so. He was through the open window in a flash, leaning over the balcony rail his eyes straining to pierce the shadows below. The sound of running footsteps echoed along the alleyway. Frank raised his Colt and as a shadowy form scurried through the gloom he squeezed the trigger. The shot shattered the night but the poor light affected Frank's aim and before he could fire again the figure disappeared.

Frank shrugged his shoulders, slipped his Colt back into its holster and climbed back through the window. He dropped on one knee beside the silent figure and turned the man over. The sheriff gasped staring wide-eyed at the dead man. 'Mal Clements!' he gasped incredulously. Frank's thoughts raced. Why had Clements called on him? Had he changed his mind about the marriage? Who was the man in the alley? His brain pounded so that he was hardly aware of the noise in the corridor.

Hurrying footsteps and excited voices grew louder. Frank glanced up as people crowded in the doorway. Someone held a lamp high and Frank saw Jake Warren step forward.

'Heard a shot...' Warren cut his sentence short staring incredulously at Mal Clements. As Frank rose slowly to his feet Warrant looked hard at the young sheriff.

Jake Warren moved like lightning and before Frank could stop him he jerked Frank's Colt from its holster. He felt the barrel and sniffed at the muzzle. The sheriff knew Warren's thoughts before he voiced them and he realised how bad his position must look.

'He was dead when I came in,' said Frank. 'I fired at the killer as he made his get-away down the alley.'

'Who is it?' Whose been killed?' Cowboys and girls crowding the doorway shouted the question.

'Mal Clements!' called Warren.

A murmur ran through the crowd. Clements was a well-known and well-liked man in Santa Rosa and everyone was shaken by his violent end. Suddenly the crowd was aware that Jake Warren was speaking and gradually the noise subsided. His compelling voice made them hang on to every word.

'Looks rather bad fer you, McCoy; Clements dead in your room and you with a recently fired Colt in your holster.'

'I fired at the killer,' shouted Frank angered by the implications of Warren's words.

'There's only your word fer thet,' replied Warren mockingly.

'I'd no reason to kill Clements,' stormed Frank.

'Hadn't you?' queried the rancher suavely. 'Guess I must hev been hearin' things when you were quarrelling with him this morning. Somethin' about not lettin' you marry his daughter, wasn't it?'

The crowd gasped and everyone started shouting at once. The seeds of suspicion had been skilfully sown by Warren and the crowd responded.

'Take him to jail!'

'No, deal with him ourselves!'

'Hangin's too good fer him!'

A cowboy shoved his way forward and Frank drew a sharp breath as he recognised him.

'Clay Duncan!' he hissed. 'So you did double back.'

'Yeah,' grinned Clay, 'but you shore made us go a long way. Thought you weren't goin' to give up followin' us. I see you've tagged who we are since we last met.' His voice was quiet, only meant for Frank and Jake Warren and now, as Clay grinned at Jake, Frank knew that Clements' suspicion had been correct. Suddenly Duncan grabbed Frank's shirt and jerked him forward. 'I don't like a sheriff whose a murderer!' he yelled. He pushed Frank towards the door. 'Take him to jail!'

Angry shouts rose from the cowboys as they grasped at the sheriff propelling him forward through their midst. In vain he tried to make himself heard. His Stetson was knocked from his head; fists pummelled his back and ribs; blows were aimed at his head and when he reached the top of the stairs a boot in the small of his back sent him tumbling to the bottom with a crash. Slowly he dragged himself to his feet, blood streaming from his face. The howling mob tore down the stairs and swept him through the lobby into the street.

Word of the killing had spread like fire through Santa Rosa and already a crowd was gathering on the main street. Suddenly Frank felt afraid. It seemed as if every man's hand had turned against him. He felt like some cornered animal waiting for the final blow to be struck. His brain pounded and the yells of the crowd, which closed in on him as he was pushed and jostled towards the jail, were deafening in his ears. Suddenly he was aware that Jake Warren and Clay Duncan were on either side of him pushing would be attackers away, and to some measure protecting him. Frank was puzzled; he hadn't time to reason things out but he soon had his answer.

They reached the front of the sheriff's office where Frank saw Mark Stevens, his deputy, crowded by the mob and unable to do anything to help him. People were yelling for a rope when Jake Warren jumped on to the sidewalk. He held his arms high calling to the crowd to be quiet. Gradually the yells died down and the murmur ran out of the crowd.

'Mal Clements was murdered this evening,' shouted Warren. 'We found the sheriff beside the body, a warm Colt in his holster!' Yells interrupted Warren but as they subsided he continued. 'Of course, the sheriff says he's innocent and has an explanation.' The crowd laughed derisively. 'If that is so, then I say he should have a fair trial. We mustn't take the law into our own hands.'

Warren paused allowing his words to sink in and have the desired effect. The crowd murmured amongst themselves. Here and there angry shouts arose yelling for the sheriff's blood. The mob had been worked up to a lynching but now Warren was trying to reason with them. The crowd started to argue amongst itself as the cool sense of reason made itself felt in some minds.

The rancher smiled to himself. 'If we judge McCoy ourselves and use that rope,' he yelled, 'we'll all be guilty of an outrageous crime and should stand trial ourselves.' He paused a moment. Men looked questioningly at each other and began to nod their agreement. 'I say we should keep him in jail until the judge comes,' he shouted. Murmurs of assent moved slowly through the crowd as men realised they had been saved from an ugly situation.

Frank was puzzled. If Warren wanted him out of the way he had the golden opportunity. He had incited the mob, but now he was calming them down. What game was Warren playing?

'We can't leave McCoy in the hands of his deputy,' continued Warren, 'that would be unfair to Mark Stevens; he would be torn between loyalty to the sheriff and a sense of duty; so I propose we elect someone else temporarily.'

Frank gasped as the crowd roared their approval. How quickly this smooth-tongued rancher had swung the mob round to agree with him. He was winning their admiration and setting himself up as a fair-minded man who wanted to see justice. Frank was beginning to realise that the whole thing had been carefully planned by Warren to get Clements and himself out of the way at the same time setting himself up as the man in authority. With only Abbe left, it would be easy for Warren to move in to Santa Rosa whenever he wished.

Suddenly Frank started; Abbe was pushing her way frantically through the crowd. Pushing, struggling, elbowing, she fought her way to the front but firm hands held her back as she tried to force her way up the steps to Frank. He saw in her eyes a wild, frightened, bewildered look, but one which didn't accuse him. He shook his head and saw trust and belief come back in her look. He felt relieved that at least she believed in him even though her father lay dead in his room.

'I have a suggestion,' yelled Warren. 'Who ever takes over the job of sheriff temporarily should be neutral. There are two such men here, Clay Duncan an' Ed Mason. They were passin' through but maybe they'll stay to see this through for us.'

Again the crowd yelled its approval. Frank attempted to speak but was howled down and Mark who tried to object fared no better.

'That's settled then,' yelled Warren with pleasure. 'Git this murderer under lock an' key.'

As Frank was pushed towards the office door he stumbled against Mark. 'It's a frame-up,' he whispered urgently, 'Abbe's in danger, get her to my brother.'

A puzzled look crossed Mark's face as he was shoved to one side. Events had moved so swiftly that they had bewildered the young deputy and he had been unable to halt them in favour of the sheriff.

Frank was bundled through the office to the cells and as the barred door clanged behind him he flopped wearily on to the bunk hoping that Mark had understood his message.

Chapter Three

As Frank disappeared through the office door Abbe tore herself free from the restraining hands. She rushed up the steps but Jake Warren's powerful arms barred her path.

'I wouldn't go in there if I was you,' he said quietly, holding her firmly.

Abbe looked at him wildly her eyes red with tears. 'I can't believe he did it; Frank couldn't,' she shouted struggling to free herself.

'But I saw him bendin' over your father, his gun still warm,' replied Jake. 'I know it must be a shock to you. I'm sure you'd be wiser to go home. I'll git one of my men to escort you.' Warren relaxed his grip and started to shove his way through a group of people who still crowded close to the sheriff's office.

Released from the detaining hands Abbe stepped towards the office, but was halted as a firm hand gripped her arm. Wide-eyed and frightened she turned swiftly to see Mark Stevens.

'Quick, Miss Abbe, you're in danger, come

with me,' he whispered.

Although Abigail had been determined to see Frank there was something compelling in the urgent tone of the voice and the girl felt reassurance as Mark gripped her hand and led her through the crowd which was beginning to disperse.

A hundred yards along the street Mark turned into an alleyway and halted to give Abbe a quick explanation.

'Frank bumped into me as they took him inside; he whispered it was a frame-up, thet you were in danger an' I was to take you to his brother.'

Abbe gasped. 'Red Springs in Texas! But I can't leave here. Frank's in trouble and I'll have to run things now dad's been...' Her voice faltered and she shuddered at the thought of her father's violent end.

'Maybe thet's why Frank wants you to git out of town,' replied Mark urgently. 'With you takin' over now your father's dead maybe Frank sees danger from Warren. If Warren killed your father an' framed Frank then you're the only one left in his way – an' Warren was eager to hev you escorted home!' added Mark half to himself as he began to see the events of the night more clearly.

A yell from the end of the street startled them. 'Miss Clements! Anyone seen Miss Clements?' They recognised Warren's voice, urgent and anxious. Mark pressed Abbe closer into the deep shadows, his hand easing his Colt in its holster. An anxious moment passed before they heard the voices move along the main street but it gave Abigail time to realise the full significance of Mark's words and to understand something of Frank's suspicions.

'Maybe you're right,' she whispered, 'but what about Frank?'

'He'll be safe enough until the judge gits here in two weeks' time. Warren won thet bunch over by seeming to uphold justice an' he won't want to spoil thet impression. I'll git you to Red Springs an' Frank's brother an' I'll return to clear up this mess.'

'When do we leave?' asked Abbe.

'Right away,' replied Mark. 'It'll be better if I don't go fer my horse; hev you two at home?'

Abbe nodded.

'C'm on, let's ride before Warren really turns on the search,' said Mark and led the way quickly along the alley.

'Shorty! Clem!' called Warren as he moved

33

away from Abbe and pushed his way through the crowd.

The two cowboys elbowed their way towards him.

'Escort Miss Clements home,' he ordered. 'An' stay with her until I git there.'

The two men nodded and fell in behind Warren as he turned round. Reaching the top of the steps he found Abbe was no longer there. He looked round anxiously searching the crowds but there was no sign of Abbe. He cursed angrily and spinning on his heels he flung open the door of the sheriff's office.

'Where's Miss Clements,' he shouted as he strode into the room.

Clay Duncan and Ed Mason looked puzzled. 'No one came in here,' said Clay.

Warren cursed himself for letting Abbe out of his sight. He stormed out of the office and rejoined Shorty and Clem on the sidewalk.

'She's gone,' snapped Warren glancing angrily up and down the street. 'C'm on; we must find her,' he snarled and started along the boards.

Warren regained his composure as he moved amongst the people still lingering in small groups. 'Anyone seen Miss Clements?' he kept asking, hiding his annoyance at her disappearance. He paused and glanced casually along an alleyway. He turned to his sidekicks. 'Search the alley,' he ordered quietly but as they stepped forward he halted them. 'Wait, we're wasting our time. She'll head fer home; git out to the Clements' house an' watch out fer Miss Clements. I'll be at the sheriff's office. Let me know as soon as she returns and see she doesn't leave until I git there.'

'Leave it to us, boss,' muttered Clem.

The two cowboys hurried towards the darkness at the edge of the town. They approached the house cautiously and finding it deserted they settled down to wait in the shadows on the verandah.

Mark guided Abbe swiftly through the side streets and alleys of Santa Rosa working all the time towards the Clements' house on the edge of town.

'We'll swing round and approach it from the back,' he whispered as the dark outline of the house loomed in the blackness.

The girl nodded and they circled the house carefully.

'Don't see anyone about,' said Abbe quietly.

'Can't be too careful,' replied Mark. 'Wait

here, I'll hev a look round.'

'Be careful,' whispered Abbe and Mark patted her hand comfortingly before slipping away into the darkness towards the house.

He moved silently and cautiously towards the back door and reached it without trouble. He drew his Colt and inched his way along the wall towards the corner. He peered round carefully and drew back sharply when he saw the outlines of two men sitting on the verandah. Mark cursed his luck. If these were Warren's men then Frank must have been right about the rancher and Warren had played fast guessing that Abbe might return home. The young deputy paused a moment formulating his plan.

Swiftly and silently he stepped round the corner.

'Keep your hands off those Colts,' he snapped. The two cowboys gasped with surprise. 'An' don't turn round,' rapped Mark viciously. The two men froze where they were. 'Right,' continued Mark calmly, 'jest ease yourselves up.' The two men rose slowly to their feet. 'Now, unbuckle your gun belts.'

The men hesitated for a moment before doing as they were told. The gunbelts clattered to the floor before Mark spoke again.

'Now, back up slowly to me, one at a time.'

The two men glanced helplessly at each other. Clem moved first, shuffling slowly backwards his feet scraping along the wood. As he neared the young deputy, Mark raised his Colt and brought the barrel crashing down upon Clem's head. Without a groan the cowboy sank to the boards.

'Right,' snapped Mark, 'now you.'

As Shorty moved backwards Mark stepped over the silent form at his feet and quickly sent Shorty to join his companion. Satisfied with his work Mark moved swiftly round the house and after making certain that there were no more of Warren's side-kicks about he hurried back to Abbe.

'Two of them,' he informed her, 'but they won't trouble us anymore. C'm on, we must be quick.' They hurried to the house. 'Get a few things together,' instructed Mark, 'whilst I tie these hombres up an' saddle the horses.'

'You'll find some rope in the stables,' replied Abbe and entered the house.

Mark soon found the rope and after securely fastening the unconscious men he dragged them to the stable where he quickly saddled two horses. Bolting and barring the door he led them to the verandah rail.

'Miss Abbe,' he called as he went into the house, 'are you ready?'

In answer to his call a door closed and footsteps hurried lightly across the landing and down the stairs. He saw that Abigail had changed into a more suitable attire for the journey. Dark jeans folded neatly into the top of brown riding boots accentuated her slim figure. A dark green blouse was covered by a warm matching vest. A shallow-crowned, narrow-brimmed sombrero hung from a cord around her neck around which a yellow neckerchief was tied. Abbe carried a thick short-length, sheepskin coat and a roll of blankets.

They hurried to the kitchen and soon had the saddle bags packed with food for the journey. A few minutes later with sadness in her heart Abbe swung into the saddle and rode from the house with Mark at her side facing a journey of over three hundred miles to Red Springs, Texas.

Jake Warren paced the sheriff's office impatiently. 'Two hours an' still no word from Shorty,' he snapped angrily. 'What's keepin' them?'

Clay Duncan flicked his Stetson to the back of his head with his thumb, tilted his chair on its two back legs, swung his feet on to the desk and continued to pick his teeth with a matchstick. He observed Warren with a twinkle of amusement in his eyes.

'Stop worryin',' he drawled. 'I figure thet gal may hev gone to some friends or relations.'

'She has no relations,' snapped Warren.

'Wal, friends then,' replied Clay testily. 'Sit down an' relax, everythin's goin' your way. The gal will sell out an' if she doesn't then...' He patted his gun and grinned evilly.

'Same as her father,' laughed Ed. 'This has been an easy job fer us, eh Clay?'

Clay grinned back at him. 'Shore has.'

Warren flung himself into a chair. 'It may not be finished yet, you stick around as arranged.'

'Hev some coffee, Mister Warren,' said Ed. 'If Miss Clements has gone to friends then you'll hev a long wait 'til daylight.'

The night passed too slowly for Warren. He dozed and woke with a start several times thinking he heard someone coming but each time the footsteps clattered past the sheriff's office. Impatiently he watched the dawn move along the Pecos Valley and fill Santa Rosa with a new day but still there was no sign of the expected cowboys.

'Git over to Betsy's,' Warren said to Duncan indicating the café across the street. 'Git your breakfast an' bring some back fer McCoy. Ed, you stay here! I'm goin' fer a shave an' we'll hev breakfast when I git back. If we haven't heard from Shorty by then we'll find out what's happened.' Warren picked up his Stetson and left the office.

Although refreshed by his shave and breakfast Jake Warren was in no better mood as he re-crossed the street with Ed Mason to the sheriff's office.

'Clay, hang on here, Ed an' I are goin' over to Clements' place.' Warren swung back through the door, climbed into the saddle and with Ed Mason beside him rode at a quick trot towards the edge of the town.

As they approached Clements' house Warren surveyed it through narrowed eyes. There was no sign of Shorty nor Clem. The rancher and his hired gunman swung slowly from their saddles in front of the house. They walked slowly towards the front door, their eyes probing everywhere, suspicion filling their minds when no one greeted them.

'I don't like it,' muttered Warren as he tried the front door and found it locked. 'Where's Shorty an' Clem? Let's take a look around.'

The two men walked slowly round the house but failed to find any trace of the missing cowboys.

'Thet leaves the stable,' snapped Warren irritated by the disappearance of his side-kicks.

Followed by Ed Mason he hurried across to the wooden building, raised the bar and flung open the door. Daylight flooded into the stable to reveal two figures securely tied to the wall. Jake cursed as he leaped forward pulling a knife from his pocket. He cut Shorty's ropes whilst Ed released Clem and as Warren untied the gag round Shorty's face he questioned them angrily.

'What happened?' he asked, his eyes blazing.

The two cowboys told their story as they rubbed the circulation back into their wrists and ankles. In no mood to tell the story pleasantly they heaped curses on Mark Stevens' head.

Warren's face darkened with anger and annoyance as he paced up and down. 'We didn't reckon on the loyalty of a deputy,' he said furiously. 'Any idea where they headed?'

The two cowboys shook their heads. 'I remember very hazily the two horses dis-appearing through the stable door,' answered Shorty. 'It was sometime after thet thet I heard them move away.'

'Must hev been preparin' fer a long journey,' commented Ed Mason.

'Could be,' replied Warren thoughtfully. 'But where? Why should Abbe Clements ride far with Mark Stevens unless they've formed some suspicions?' His eyes narrowed. 'We've got to find them!' he said, his voice vibrating with a passionate determination.

'They sounded to head south, away from town,' offered Shorty.

'Could hev circled,' pointed out Ed Mason.

'Hardly likely they'd waste time,' commented Warren. 'Stevens would figure I'd sent Shorty an' Clem. Reckon he'd put as much ground as possible between us before I came searchin'. C'm on we'll git back to town.'

The four men hurried to the horses and riding two up on each horse returned to the sheriff's office.

'Shorty an' Clem stay here,' ordered Warren. 'An' see that no one pulls anythin' on you again. We don't want to lose McCoy. Clay an' Ed ride with me.'

After hasty preparations Jake Warren and his two hired guns swung into the saddles and sent their horses at a fast gallop out of Santa Rosa.

They turned on to the south road and guided by firm hands the horses stretched themselves in a swift rhythmic gallop. The three riders did not speak and the miles were covered quickly.

Five miles from Santa Rosa the trail forked and Warren slowed down as he neared the dilapidated building, which had once boasted of being a ranch-house, standing near the trail. The dust swirled around the hoofs as the horses milled around in front of the broken verandah.

'Silas, you there, Silas,' bellowed Warren.

A few moments passed before the door opened slowly and an old man shuffled out shielding his eyes against the glare of the sun.

'Silas,' snapped Warren, 'hev you seen two riders, man an' woman, pass through here durin' the night?'

The old man hesitated a moment, puckered his brow, his eyes narrowing as he looked up as if trying to make out who was speaking.

'Speak up, you drunken crawler,' snarled Warren impatiently.

'Ho, it' you Mister Warren,' slurred the old

man pulling at his dirty, tattered clothes, as if to apologise for his appearance. His eyes sharpened when he realised who sat on the horse. He glanced penetratingly at the two men alongside Warren his eyes missing nothing. He looked back at the dark-haired rancher. 'Maybe there was; maybe there wasn't,' he muttered half to himself but with sufficient emphasis for the riders to hear. He rubbed his stubbled chin. 'I'll hev to see if I can remember,' he added shrewdly.

Warren's fingers searched the pocket of his vest. He pulled out a dollar and threw it in the dust at Silas's feet. 'Will thet help you to remember?' he asked between clenched teeth.

The old man's eyes brightened as he saw in the silver dollar the means of obtaining another bottle. He chuckled to himself as he bent down to pick up the coin. Straightening he looked hard at Warren seated upright on his black horse.

'Maybe it will at thet,' grinned Silas swinging from one foot to the other.

'Well git on with it,' snapped Warren impatient with the delay.

The old man was not to be hurried. 'It was dark when they passed here, but old Silas was about. I see the comin's an' goin's on this road an' I could tell you a thing or two.'

Ed Mason shoved his horse forward close to Silas and leaning from the saddle aimed a blow at the old man's head. 'Stop wastin' time an' answer Mr Warren's question,' he hissed.

Silas stepped backwards avoiding the blow. His face darkened. 'You'd better curb these sidekicks Mister Warren or I'll tell you nothin'.' His harshness eased and a crafty look came into his eyes. 'New around here ain't they? Gun-butts smooth.'

Warren signalled to Ed Mason not to interfere and ignoring Silas's remarks he threw down another dollar and waited for the information he wanted.

'Like I was sayin', Mister Warren,' continued Silas when he saw he had the upper-hand, 'these two riders passed here in the dark an' it was difficult to see whether they were man an' woman but the shorter of the two was very slim – I figure it could hev been a woman.' He stroked his dark, stubbled chin as if trying to recall the unknown riders. 'Mm, now I come to think of it I reckon it was some female.'

'Wal, which way did they go?' snapped the rancher.

'The only way anyone would go at that

time of night,' replied the old man. 'They swung towards the Pecos valley an' thet means Fort Sumner.'

Without a word Warren hauled his horse round and kicked it into a fast run. Clay and Ed were close on his heels and as the dust rose behind them, Silas chuckled to himself, gripped his dollars tightly and shuffled through the doorway.

Chapter Four

As Mark Stevens turned away from Santa Rosa he had a feeling of guilt; of deserting his friend, Frank McCoy. The impulse to turn the horse, ride back to town and attempt to rescue the sheriff was strong but he forced himself to ride ahead. It eased his mind that he was obeying Frank's urgent, whispered instructions to take Abbe away from Santa Rosa.

Mark set a fast pace wanting to put as much ground between them and the town before the two cowboys were discovered in the stable. Abbe handled her horse skilfully, keeping pace with Mark. They swung towards the Pecos and followed the river for some distance. Mark was thankful that he knew the trail well enough to make the ride in the dark and he hoped to reach Fort Sumner before stopping.

Abbe eased herself in the saddle as the trail steepened and climbed away from the river to cut across some high bluffs before dropping down to cross Alamogordo Creek.

The ride so far had been hard and fast, but she was determined not to show any sign of tiredness although the shock of the events in Santa Rosa, the murder of her father, and seeing Frank misused by the mob had sapped a great deal of her strength.

They splashed across the ford and urged their horses upwards into the hills north of Fort Sumner. The twisting trail climbed and dropped across barren hillsides into lush green valleys before swinging south to drop off the hills into the town.

'We'll rest here,' said Mark. 'I've got some friends who will take us in. It will only be a few hours to daylight but the rest will do you good.'

Abbe nodded in silence, relieved that there was to be a break in the ride. Suddenly, she felt desperately lonely, her father gone and Frank back in Santa Rosa behind bars. She felt as if she was running out on him just when she should be beside him declaring that she believed he was innocent. She opened her mouth about to ask Mark to take her back when she realised that the deputy was only obeying orders, and Frank wished her to be safe.

Only the odd light remained in the houses of Fort Sumner and Mark was pleased to see that his friends had not gone to bed. Wearily, Abbe slipped from the saddle into Mark's helping hands and soon she was warming herself by the crackling fire as May Saunders hurried to prepare a hot meal for them. May and her husband Al had been childhood friends of Mark and their smiling, open faces did much to reassure Abbe. Steaming coffee was soon ready and helped to drive out the cold of the night ride, whilst Mark quickly told his friends of the happenings in Santa Rosa.

'I feel sure Warren will soon be on our trail, might even be ridin' south now. We must hev an early start in the morning,' he urged. 'I'll take the horses to the livery stables an' arrange fer fresh ones in the morning.'

Al accompanied Mark and soothed his neighbour irritated at having to turn out of his bed. After making the necessary arrangements the two men returned to the house where Abbe was already enjoying the hot meal which May had set in front of her.

The weariness of the ride, the warmth of the room, and hunger appeased, Abbe soon felt sleepy and once she was between clean, fresh sheets, she was soon fast asleep. She seemed to have been asleep for hours when she woke suddenly wondering where she was. The events of the past evening poured wearily back to her and sleep now became fitful to her troubled mind, but before daylight came she had reached an important decision.

Light fell across Mark's face to waken him. He rolled over tempted to go back to sleep, but the urgency of the new day hurried him from his bunk.

Abbe was already enjoying her breakfast when Mark entered the room and the smile with which she greeted him told him she was greatly refreshed by her sleep.

'Glad to see you lookin' better,' said Mark. 'You've a long ride ahead. I want you to git started as soon as possible. May, where's Al?'

'He's just gone over to the stable, he'll be back in a moment,' replied May.

Abbe looked curiously at Mark. 'What do you mean, Mark?' she asked. 'You talk as if you weren't coming.'

The young cowboy bit his lip before speaking as if weighing up his words. 'I'm not!' he announced. He paused, embarrassed by the way Abbe and May stared incredulously at him. He realised he had put his words badly and hastened to reassure them. 'I'm not desertin' you but I think I should return to Santa Rosa and try to help Frank. I'm goin' to ask Al to take you to Red Springs.' He saw the tension in the two women relax and relief sweep across their faces.

'Mark,' said Abbe leaning forward on the table, 'I too came to a decision last night. I was wondering how to tell you but you spoke first. I'm not going to Red Springs; I'm goin' back to Santa Rosa. I can no more desert Frank than you can.'

Protestations sprang to May's lips as she stepped to Abbe's side, but Abbe would not listen to them.

'Frank wanted you to be safe,' pointed out Mark, 'an' I think he'd be easier in his mind if he knew you were. I also think he believed his brother would help him.'

'Exactly,' said Abbe eagerly. 'Al can still go to Red Springs; we'll go back to Santa Rosa.' She halted the argument almost before Mark spoke. 'Let me finish,' she said. 'Don't you see that if Jake Warren knows I'm somewhere about it's going to embarrass him; it's going to throw him into the open. If I go to Red Springs he'll do as he likes with my property, but if I am around he's going to have to be more careful.'

Mark saw the determination in the pretty

young face, and he knew it was useless to argue and had to admit there was something in what she said.

When Al returned they told him of their decision and he eagerly offered his help. He prepared for his long ride whilst Mark hurried to the livery stables.

'Shan't need fresh horses, now,' he informed the stableman. 'Our own will do.'

The old man grunted, accepted payment for the night's stabling and turned to his work. The deputy hurried back to the house and after thanking his friends Mark and Abbe bade them farewell and left Fort Sumner by the north road.

They put their horses into a steady trot and were soon climbing into the hills. They resisted the temptation to force their mounts faster knowing it was better to conserve some energy for the unknown ahead. At every bend and rise Mark proceeded cautiously fearing that Warren might be riding south on their trail.

They moved steadily through the hills and as they topped the rise above Alamogordo Creek Mark pulled his horse to a halt. Suddenly he jerked the animal round, grabbed Abbe's horse by the bridle and pulled it after him. Once below the skyline he stopped.

'Riders approachin' the Creek,' he explained to the startled girl as he stepped from the saddle. He crept quickly to the top of the hill and removing his Stetson peered cautiously over the rise.

His eyes narrowed. Water flew as three horsemen urged their mounts across the Creek. Mark watched them push the animals faster once they reached the bank and started the climb up the hillside. Suddenly, he gasped and turning raced back to Abbe who held their horses steady.

'Warren an' two sidekicks,' he panted glancing desperately around. 'Quick, over to those rocks,' he instructed pointing to a clump of rocks about a quarter of a mile away.

Abbe heeled her horse forward as Mark swung into the saddle to send his horse pounding across the hillside. When they reached the cover of the rocks Mark hurled himself from the saddle and threw his reins to Abbe before sliding his rifle from the leather.

'Keep 'em quiet,' he called and scrambled up a flat slope of rock to an advantageous position between two boulders.

The minutes seemed like hours as he waited. Suddenly, he stiffened. Jake Warren topped the rise and pulled his horse to a halt. Mark's eyes narrowed and his lips tightened in a thin line when he saw Clay Duncan and Ed Mason draw alongside Warren. The three riders looked around before the rancher pointed downwards. The two gunmen nodded and as one the three men kicked their horses into a full gallop in the direction of Fort Sumner.

Mark breathed more freely as he watched them go, but waited until they were out of sight before sliding down the rock to Abbe.

'They've headed for Fort Sumner,' reported Mark. 'We must ride hard; they'll soon find we've left an' there may be a chance of rescuin' Frank before they get back to Santa Rosa.'

'Then let's ride,' said Abbe eagerly.

They climbed into the saddles, crossed the top of the hill and sent their horses into a fast slithering, slide down the slope to Alamogordo Creek. Once across the water they urged their horses faster and hardly a word was spoken as they followed the trail which twisted its way through the hills bordering the Pecos River.

As the wind sang in her ears Abbe felt some measure of relief and happiness in the fact that she was returning to Santa Rosa and facing her troubles instead of running away from them. Mark, grim-faced, was lost in his thoughts of outwitting the men guarding Frank before Warren returned.

The trail slipped down from the hills towards the river and turned towards Santa Rosa before Mark eased the pace. He moved closer to Abbe.

'I'm goin' to try to bluff this out,' he said. 'Townsfolk won't know Warren's after us an' providin' we don't run into any of his cowpokes I may be able to git into the jail without raisin' suspicion.'

Abbe smiled. 'It may work. What do you want me to do?'

'We must hev fresh horses an' some more food if possible,' replied Mark.

'We can get more food from home, but horses...' She looked thoughtful as she paused. Suddenly she brightened. 'Can't we get them from the livery stable?'

'Why not,' agreed Mark excitedly. 'There's no reason why old Marner should be suspicious. I'll leave you to get the food whilst I get the horses.'

They turned off the trail and headed for the Clements house. Mark's eyes probed everywhere, suspicious that Warren may have left some guards, but they remained unchallenged. He checked the house and other buildings quickly and when he was satisfied that all was well he called Abbe and escorted her inside.

Abbe busied herself preparing for the exile she knew must follow if they released Frank. Mark remounted and took the two dust-covered, sweating horses to the livery stables.

'Howdy, Mark,' greeted old Marner as the deputy rode in. 'Looks as if you've been ridin' some,' he added eyeing the weary animals.

'Yeah,' answered Mark cautiously. 'I want you to take charge of these two an' let me have other three.'

Old Marner glanced sharply at the lawman. He rubbed his chin thoughtfully. 'I'm not sure thet I can,' he said slowly.

Mark stiffened. Had Warren started to exert his authority already by ordering Marner not to hire horses? The young deputy looked suspiciously at the leather-faced old man.

'I must hev them,' answered Mark forcefully.

'You must aim on doin' a lot of ridin',' muttered the stableman.

'Maybe I do,' replied Mark testily. 'Now, can I hev them?'

'Guess so,' said the old man somewhat reluctantly. 'It'll leave me short but I guess your money's as good as anyone else's.'

Mark felt relieved as he followed Marner along the stable.

'Better take those,' said Marner indicating three good looking animals.

Mark examined them quickly but carefully and satisfied that they were all right he soon had them saddled and bridled. He paid Marner and hurried back to the Clements house. Abbe had everything ready and after Mark had selected two rifles from the study they quickly loaded the horses.

'What is the plan?' asked Abbe when they had finished.

'I hope to take whoever's in the office by surprise. You be at the back of the jail with three horses,' answered Mark.

Abbe nodded. 'I'll be waiting,' she said.

They swung into the saddles but before turning their horses away from the house Mark looked seriously at Abbe. 'Have you a gun?' he asked grimly.

The girl fumbled in the pocket of her jeans. 'I have this,' she replied pulling out a small pearl-handled gun.

'Good,' said Mark. 'If anythin' should go wrong head for Fort Sumner an' contact

May. Al will be bringin' Frank's brother an he'll look after you.'

Abbe's eyes clouded. She looked pleadingly at Mark. 'Nothing must go wrong,' she whispered, 'nothing, Frank must be rescued.'

Mark smiled encouragingly and they kicked their horses forward to head for town. They kept to the side streets moving cautiously nearer the sheriff's office and jail. A block from the jail Mark drew rein, slipped from the saddle and handed Abbe the reins.

'Wait at the back of the jail,' he instructed, 'but give me time to get inside before you take up position.'

Abbe nodded; her heart pounded, her throat dried, she could not speak. The deputy smiled, swung on his heels and hurried along a narrow alley leading to Main Street. He slowed to a casual walk as he reached the end of the alley and sauntered round the corner. He strolled slowly along the sidewalk. Cowboys nodded to him as they passed and he acknowledged their greeting as if everything in Santa Rosa was as it should be. The urge to break into a run was strong but he held himself in check. He was anxious for Abbe's sake and he hoped no one decided to use the back road. Three horses packed for a long journey and held by Abigail Clements near the back door of the jail were rather obvious of someone's intentions, but that was a risk they had to take.

Mark reached the door of the sheriff's office and paused a moment to make sure that there were none of Jake Warren's cow-pokes along the street. Satisfied that he would not be troubled from that side he opened the door and stepped inside swiftly, drawing his Colt as he did so.

Shorty and Clem, who were sitting beside the desk gasped when they saw Mark with the cold muzzle of a Colt facing them.

'Git on your feet,' snarled Mark.

The two men glanced at each other and slowly pushed themselves from the chairs. Shorty opened his mouth to speak but Mark silenced him as he snapped– 'Unbuckle your gun belts.' Clem and Shorty hesitated. 'Move,' rapped the lawman. The two men unfastened their belts and their guns thudded to the floor.

'Raise your hands, turn around an' march for the cells,' ordered Mark.

As they moved forward he removed the key to the cells from its hook on the wall. Frank McCoy leaped from the bunk with a yell when he saw Warren's sidekicks enter the cell block with their hands raised.

'Mark!' he gasped with astonishment. 'Good work.' Eagerly he gripped the bars as he watched his deputy move carefully round the humiliated cowboys and insert the key in the lock. His eyes never left the two men and his gun never wavered. A sharp turn of the key and Frank pushed the cell door open quickly.

'All right, you two, inside quick,' snapped Mark, 'an' keep your backs to me.'

They shuffled forward and once inside the cell Mark crashed the barrel of his Colt across Shorty's head. Clem half turned as he saw Shorty's knees buckle but Mark swiftly despatched him to the floor. The lawman slipped his gun back into its holster, slammed the cell door shut and pocketed the key after relocking the door.

'Out the back,' said Mark as Frank reappeared from the office buckling on a gun belt.

Mark flung open the door and as Frank stepped outside he gasped in amazement.

'Abbe!'

'Frank!' Abbe's greeting relieved all the pent up feelings and nerves when she saw the man she loved.

'Thought I told you to take her to Texas,' grinned Frank unable to be annoyed now that he was free and with Abbe again.

'Tell you about it later,' replied Mark climbing into the leather. 'Let's git out of here first.'

Frank was already swinging into the saddle. The three friends threaded their way through the side streets of Santa Rosa and reaching the edge of town without being seen headed west at a fast gallop.

Chapter Five

Three dust-covered men eased the pace of their sweating horses when they reached the main street of Fort Sumner. They rode close together their eyes searching for some sign of the cowboy and girl they were trailing.

'Livery stable might help,' said Jake Warren curtly.

Clay Duncan and Ed Mason grunted their approval as they turned their mounts towards the wooden building which housed the town's stable. They stepped down from the saddles and the two hired gunmen placed themselves in an advantageous position to survey the street whilst Jake Warren went inside.

'Mornin',' greeted the stableman as he eyed the dust-covered stranger.

'Good mornin',' answered Warren pleasantly. 'I'm lookin' fer a friend of mine. Thought you might be able to help me.'

'Will if I can,' grunted the older man.

'Young fellah, probably rode in here last night, maybe had a girl with him.'

'Ain't hed a gal in here,' replied the stable-man shaking his head.

'Hev you had any strangers in?' asked Warren pulling a ten dollar bill from his pocket.

A smile flicked across the man's face as he accepted the money.

'There was a young fellah, brought two horses in but he's gone again.'

'When?' asked Warren eagerly.

'This mornin'.'

'Know where he headed?' Warren sensed he was on to something and he pressed his question again.

The older man scratched his head. 'Don't rightly know, never said.' He looked shrewdly at Warren who was not slow to notice a twinkle in the man's eyes and guessed that he was holding something back. Another bill exchanged hands. 'There was somethin' strange about his goin',' he added. 'Last night he said he'd want fresh horses to-day but this mornin' he took the same two. Guess he must hev changed his mind about where he was goin'.'

Warren's eyes lit up with a smile. 'Thet helps a lot,' he said. 'Thanks, old timer,' he added as he swung on his heels and left the stable.

'Any news?' asked Clay as the rancher reappeared.

'Left this mornin',' replied Warren. 'I reckon it was them. Stranger came in here last night with two horses, wanted two fresh ones this mornin'.'

'Which way did they go?' asked Ed.

'Don't know,' said Warren, 'but I'm goin' to play a hunch. This fellah didn't take the fresh horses so he must hev changed his mind about where he was goin' an' takin' the same animals I reckon he could be headin' back where he came from.'

'Santa Rosa?' said Clay incredulously.

'Yeah. Why not?' asked Warren.

The hired gunmen looked at each other with surprise and shrugged their shoulders. 'Could be,' they agreed.

'C'm on then let's ride,' said Warren.

The three men gathered the reins, swung into the saddles and turning their mounts stirred the dust as they left Fort Sumner at a fast clip.

Hardly a word was spoken on the four hour ride to Santa Rosa. Warren forced the pace hard and did not spare the horses.

'Clements' house,' he shouted as they neared the town. The three riders turned their horses from the trail and soon pulled to a dust raising halt in front of the house. Warren flung himself from the saddle and hurried into the house whilst Mason and Duncan circled the building.

'No sign of 'em,' said Clay Duncan when they met Warren emerging from the house.

'There is. They've been in here,' answered the rancher striding from the verandah. 'C'm on let's see if they've been seen in town.'

They sprang on to their horses and kicked them into a gallop. Curious heads turned as the three dust-covered men pounded down the main street and hauled their horses to a halt in front of the sheriff's office. They slipped quickly from the saddles, crossed the sidewalk and flung open the office door.

'What the...?' Warren's gasp of surprise at finding the room empty was halted by a moan from the cells. Four quick steps took him to the cells. 'Shorty! Clem!' he gasped when he saw his two sidekicks struggling to their feet. He leaped to the cell door but found it locked. 'Mason, shoot the lock open,' he ordered.

Ed Mason drew his Colt and pointing the barrel close to the lock squeezed the trigger. The shot reverberated round the building and as the pungent smoke cleared they saw the lock was shattered. Clay Duncan jerked the door open and Warren stepped inside followed by the two hired gunmen. They dragged Shorty and Clem to the office where they flopped into two chairs holding their damaged heads.

'Git the doc,' ordered Warren and Clay Duncan hurried to find him. 'There's a flask of brandy in my saddle bag, Ed,' he added. Ed nodded and was soon back with the spirit. Warren poured each of his men a stiff drink, and as it hit their throats it helped to clear their muddled brains.'

'What happened?' snarled Warren through tight, angry lips.

'Mark Stevens ... got the drop on us...' spluttered Shorty. He looked anxiously at his boss fearing the wrath he saw in the dark face.

'Fools! Fools!' stormed Warren pacing the room. 'Call yourselves men! This is twice this slip of a deputy has outwitted you.'

'But boss...' Clem's protest was cut short.

'Never mind the excuses,' snarled Warren. 'Know where they went?'

Shorty shook his aching head. 'Didn't say anythin' to give it away,' he uttered dejectedly.

'Was the girl with him?'

'Nope.'

'Guess they'd pick her up somewhere,' Warren muttered half to himself. 'When did this happen?'

'About half an hour ago,' answered Clem.

'They can't have got far,' said Warren. He spun on his heels as the door opened to admit the doctor and Clay. 'Doc, patch these two up. Clay, Ed, we ride again.'

The three men hurried from the office, clattered across the boards and climbed into the saddles but before they could send their horses forward their attention was held by the pounding hoofs of a hard ridden horse hitting the town. When he saw the three horsemen the lone cowboy hauled his horse to a sliding, dust-raising halt in front of Jake Warren.

'What's wrong, Red?' asked Warren anxiously.

As he tried to hold his lively horse steady the cowboy replied breathlessly 'I was ridin' the western boundary when I saw three riders. I took a closer look an' saw it was McCoy, Stevens an' Miss Clements. They were in a mighty big hurry an' I knew thet McCoy should hev been in jail so I rode straight here fer you.'

'Good work, Red,' smiled the rancher.

'This'll save time. Where were they headin'?'

'Hill country,' answered the cowboy. 'My guess would be around Pintada Mesa.'

'Let's ride,' shouted Warren and pulled his horse round to head for the west road out of Santa Rosa. Three men kicked their horses after Warren and dust whirled as they pounded the trail out of town.

After riding for a mile they turned towards the hills and the dusty trail cut through the grasslands which grew thinner as they climbed steadily. In the distance the Rocky Mountains rose range after range. Their purple vastness topped with snow was in marked contrast to the barren dryness of the desert which lay before them marked by the grotesquely shaped hills and mesas which sprang from the sparse country.

Pintada Mesa rose gaunt and strange, its cliff-like side rising almost sheer. Caves marked the eastern face and a few paths to the top were known to only a handful of men. Local Mexicans avoided Pintada saying it was haunted by the ghosts of a wagon train which had sought shelter near the Mesa only to find itself ambushed by Indians.

Warren realised that if McCoy and his friends reached the Mesa without being seen, it would be difficult to find them. He urged his horse faster calling to the others to keep a good look out. His eyes scanned back and forth across the landscape ahead hoping to see a tell-tale dust cloud.

'Where did you last see them?' Warren called to the cowboy who had brought the news.

'Way along this trail near where it drops into the creek,' replied Red. 'Could still be down there.'

Warren grunted and continued his search. Half a mile further on the trail twisted and climbed suddenly amongst some rocks. At the top of the rise Warren pulled his horse to a stop. In front of him the ground dropped steeply to a dried up creek and rose as steeply on the other side to the desert which climbed towards the Mesa and the mountains.

The rancher pushed his sombrero back on his head and wiped the dust and sweat from his forehead. 'Along the creek or towards Pintada?' he half whispered to himself. He shaded his eyes and began to scan the parched landscape.

A sudden yell from Ed Mason momentarily startled the horses. 'Over there!' he shouted pointing towards the Mesa.

Warren's eyes narrowed against the glare of the desert as he followed Ed's pointing finger. A cloud of dust, miniature in the distance, rose and hung on the still air. With a shout of triumph Warren shoved his horse forward slithering and sliding down the slope to the bed of the creek. The three men followed suit sending showers of stones and dust tumbling down the slope after Warren. They sent their horses across the creek and with yells urged them up the steep slope before sending them into a fast gallop towards the rising dust which indicated the progress of riders.

When Frank followed Mark through the back streets of Santa Rosa he thought only of the danger in which Abbe had placed herself. He felt he wanted to take her away from this place which during the past twenty-four hours had brought tragedy and trouble to them both. The urge to head for Texas was great but he knew that this would not solve his troubles, it would only add to them for he would be troubled all his life by the fact that he had run away, that he had left Santa Rosa to the hands of Jake Warren.

'Reckon we can hide up in Pintada an' work somethin' out from there,' called Mark.

'Right,' answered Frank. 'Where's Warren,

any idea?'

'Yeah,' grinned the deputy. 'We last saw him headin' fer Fort Sumner as we were headin' back here.'

Mark suddenly became serious. 'Warren's no fool,' he continued. 'If he finds thet we used the same horses he'll put two an' two together an' reckon we headed back here; I should hev used fresh horses. Sooner we reach Pintada the better.'

Frank turned to Abbe who rode beside him. 'You all right, darlin'?' he called.

Abbe nodded and smiled encouragingly. The three friends said no more but flattened themselves along their horses' backs. The strong animals responded to their calls and stretched themselves across the ground pounding the trail with flying hoofs.

Frank let Mark take the lead. He knew that the young deputy, born and raised in Santa Rosa, was familiar with the Mesa. The ground rose steadily, the grass becoming sparser as they rode towards the parched land rising to the mountains. Suddenly the ground broke in front of them dropping steeply to the bed of a dried up creek. Unhesitatingly Mark put his horse down the steep slope to slide to the bottom, followed by a cloud of dust. Frank pulled on the reins, glancing anxiously at Abbe who, without a pause, sent her horse after Mark. Frank gasped as the horse plunged over the edge; it seemed to stumble, lose its footing and for one brief moment Frank thought Abbe had been thrown, but her superb horsemanship righted the false foothold and amidst a swirl of stumbling stones and earth she followed Mark down.

Frank turned his horse on the rim of the creek and as it pulled at the reins he gazed over the plain towards Santa Rosa, a mere speck on the horizon. He narrowed his eyes against the glare and thought he detected a cloud of dust but in the shimmering haze rising from the grassland he knew it was easy to make a mistake. He pulled his sweating animal round and slid after Mark and Abbe who were already urging their mounts up the steep slope. Once they reached the top the three riders put their horses into an earth shaking gallop towards the Mesa.

The trail climbed steeply and their progress became slower as they climbed higher. Frank, wondering if his eyes had not deceived him, turned his head and saw the tell-tale cloud of dust now moving across the flatness behind them. He yelled to Abbe and Mark who checked their horses and turned in the saddles to see the sign of their pursuers.

'They'll hev seen our dust cloud,' shouted Frank and urged his horse onwards as the other two riders pushed their mounts forward.

Steadily Warren and his sidekicks gained on the three riders whose climb towards the Mesa became slower as the ground steepened. Suddenly a rifle spit the vastness but the distance was too great and it only served to spur Frank and his companions onwards realising how quickly the gap was closing. Mark glanced anxiously back as more shots rang out. He urged his horse onward towards a turning in the path which began to narrow quickly. They passed through a narrow cleft between two walls of rock and turned the corner. Mark slipped quickly from the saddle drawing his rifle from its leather scabbard.

As Frank and Abbe drew alongside Mark spoke quickly. 'One hundred yards further on you'll see a cleft cuttin' into another path higher up the Mesa. It's a short cut which can't be seen from here. I'll hold them off to give you a start an' then I'll join you.'

Frank started to protest but Mark halted him. 'If Abbe wasn't with us we could deal with them but you must get her to safety. I'll be all right; one man could hold off an army from here.'

The sheriff nodded. 'Good luck,' he said and urging his horse forward led Abbe towards the cleft.

Mark put his horse in the convenient shelter of some rocks and slipped back to a position from which he commanded the trail as it passed between two walls of rock. He waited impatiently, his rifle ready for the first sight of the pursuers whom he could hear calling their mounts to greater effort.

Clay Duncan was the first to appear and Mark's rifle crashed. As the bullet smashed into his shoulder Duncan crashed to the ground. His horse rose on its hind legs screaming with fright. As it spun round its flaying hoofs pounded the ground and Clay, terror in his eyes, rolled over as the hoof tore at the ground where his head had been. The frightened animal hurled down the trail scattering the three men who followed. They jumped from their horses to the cover of some rocks and opened fire at the position occupied by Mark who sent another bullet whistling over Duncan's head as he scrambled to safety nursing a shattered shoulder.

Gradually the firing eased as Warren realised they were cornered by one man. He looked round desperately seeking some way of outwitting the lone cowboy who held them up. He saw that the man had picked his position skilfully and would easily pick them off if they dared to move forward.

Mark held his fire, content to save his ammunition which he knew might be precious during the days which lay ahead. He watched the rocks below him carefully for any sign of movement.

'D'you figure he's gone?' asked Ed Mason.

Warren smiled drily. 'Try him, Ed,' he replied curtly.

Mason did not answer but eased himself flatter against the rock and cautiously peered round. Mark's rifle shattered the silence and as the bullet clipped the rock close to Mason's head the gunman jumped back to fall sprawling at Warren's feet.

The rancher laughed loudly at the sight of the fallen man. 'Satisfied?' he mocked.

Mason glared darkly at Warren as he picked himself up. Suddenly the grin vanished from Warren's face.

'We've got to git rid of him, he can hold us here whilst the other two git away.' He cursed angrily. 'You're a hired gun, Mason, any suggestions?'

'We'll hev to wait until night to move him,' replied Mason.

'Night!' stormed Warren. 'We can't. I reckon thet's Stevens up there lettin' McCoy an' the girl escape. They'll be miles away by night.' He turned to face the rocks ahead. 'Stevens!' he shouted. 'Stevens!' There was no answer. A puzzled frown creased Warren's head. 'Stevens! You're helpin' a murderer to escape, thet makes you as guilty as he is. Come down an' help us recapture him an' we'll forgit what you've done.'

Silence greeted this suggestion.

'Reckon he's gone this time,' whispered Mason. The words were hardly out of his mouth when they heard the clatter of horse's hoofs on the rock.

'C'm on,' yelled Warren. 'He's moved Clay'll be all right here 'til we git back.'

They hurled themselves at their horses, pulled them round roughly and sent them along the trail.

As he saw Mason fall Mark, deciding that Frank and Abbe would be on the hidden trail crept swiftly and silently to his horse. He grasped the reins but suddenly he froze. His face darkened and he cursed his luck for leaving too soon for now, when Warren received no answer, he would know that no one barred his path. Mark threw caution to the wind, swung into the saddle and pushed the animal forward. He soon reached the cleft which turned sharply to the right so that trail up through the rock was hidden from the entrance to the cleft.

Once out of sight Mark swung from the saddle and held his horse steady, listening to the clatter of hoofs as the three pursuers urged their animals up the Mesa.

Mark breathed more freely when he heard Warren and his sidekicks ride past. He climbed back into the saddle and sent the animal forward up the steep, narrow trail. After about twenty minutes hard climbing Mark rode out on to a ledge which swung to the left and continued to skirt the edge of the Mesa until it came out on the huge flat top of the high mound of rock. Abbe and Frank ran forward to greet him and eager, willing hands grabbed the bridle and helped Mark from the saddle.

'You all right, Mark?' asked Frank anxiously.

'Sure,' panted the deputy as he dropped to the ground. He took off his sombrero and pulling out his handkerchief wiped the sweat and dust from his face.

'What about Warren?' asked Frank.

'He rumbled I'd left sooner than I thought he would.'

'Then he'll be up here before...' Frank's alarm was allayed as Mark interrupted.

'Not for a long time. Thet trail we were on runs out half way up. He'll never find where we vanished to an' thet means back to the bottom and try one of the other paths.' Mark laughed. 'I can see Warren tiring of this game before long.'

Abbe, who had taken Mark's horse to the others, was preparing a meal and whilst they ate they discussed plans.

'I winged one of the gunmen an' I figure he'll hev to return to Santa Rosa; thet leaves Warren an' two others,' said Mark.

Frank looked thoughtful. 'I reckon if I was in Warren's shoes I'd pull down to the foot of the Mesa,' he said, 'send someone back to town, git the rest of his cowpokes out here and keep us penned up until we hev to go down.'

Abbe looked alarmed. 'Why come up here?'

Mark smiled. 'It would hev been all right if we hadn't been followed but now I reckon Frank's right so when the light starts to fade I'll take you down on the other side of the

78

Mesa and all being well we'll be away before Warren's men git here.'

Abbe's face cleared and lit up with a smile. 'We'll head for Fort Sumner, pick up Frank's brother and return to Texas.'

Frank looked at the girl in amazement. 'And let Warren git away with your property?'

Abbe looked hard at Frank who saw all the love he had ever known flash from Abbe's deep brown eyes. 'I don't care about that so long as you are safe.'

'But you can't just leave it,' protested Frank.

'I can and would to have you safe,' replied Abbe.

Frank rose slowly to his feet. He stared at the ground thoughtfully. 'Abbe, I know you mean well but it's not as easy as that. I'm sheriff of Santa Rosa; I've been framed an' I can't just run away; I've got to clear my name an' clear Santa Rosa of Warren and his gunmen.'

Abbe listened intently to Frank; tears welled in her eyes as she heard the words she did not want to hear, but knew were the only ones Frank could say if he wanted to face the future as a man. She loved him all the more for them. Abbe stood up and moved slowly towards him. She gripped his arms.

'Darling, I know how you feel; I want you safe but I want you, and not a man living with a ghost of what he should have done.'

A faint smile flicked Frank's lips. 'Thank you,' he whispered and kissed Abbe lightly full on her lips, before turning to Mark. 'When we get down head away from Santa Rosa before doubling back.'

The deputy nodded. 'We can't use Abbe's home, but maybe we can go to old Silas, he knows all the comins' an' going's around town which could be useful to us.'

Frank agreed but Abigail looked doubtful. She shook her head. 'I don't know whether Old Silas is to be trusted,' she whispered.

Chapter Six

Jake Warren kicked his horse viciously when he realised that Mark was no longer behind the rock barring their path. He was angry that they had been held up by the young deputy sheriff but he was thankful that he had found out so quickly that Mark had left his impregnable position. Close behind Warren Ed Mason and Red urged their horses faster.

Warren could not understand why Mark had left such an advantageous position so quickly; if he had remained he could have held them at bay for a long time, but now Warren reckoned that the three riders could not be so far ahead. He grinned to himself when he thought of the power which would be in his grasp once the three riders had been disposed of.

The horses' hoofs clattered on the rock and echoed from the wall of the mesa. Warren led the way round the corner throwing caution to the winds in his pursuit of Mark Stevens. No bullets met them as they rode round the bend in the trail and Warren was shaken when he saw that Mark no longer rode ahead.

Ignoring the steep, slippery path the rancher lashed his horse faster racing for the next bend in the trail. He was determined that Mark should not escape him. As they neared the turning the three men slowed their horses and drawing their Colts proceeded with more caution expecting the deputy to make another stand. They were amazed to see no one ahead. They pulled hard on their reins bringing their sweating animals to a halt.

'Where the devil has he gone?' roared Ed.

'He can't have disappeared into thin air,' snarled Warren. 'He must be somewhere about.'

Warren pulled his horse round. 'There must be some way into this Mesa,' he said. 'C'm on, let's search this rock face carefully.'

The three men rode slowly back along the trail examining the wall of rock as they went. It was cut by a number of clefts but all appeared to be insurmountable for a man, let alone a horse.

Warren cursed angrily, when after twenty minutes' search they found nothing.

'He's given us the slip,' he shouted, 'but he must have gone up the Mesa; we'd have seen him if he'd gone down. C'm on we'll get to the bottom.' Without adding any further explanation he sent his horse down the steep slope, slithering and sliding on the rocks until they reached Clay Duncan. They helped the wounded man on to his horse and were soon at the bottom of the Mesa.

The three men were close behind the rancher when he pulled his horse to a stop. Warren turned in the saddle and looked at Pintada with hatred in his eyes. This mountain of rock was stopping him from achieving his ambition of ruling the Santa Rosa country.

'They're somewhere up there,' he muttered to himself, 'and they'll not escape Jake Warren.' He turned to Red. 'Take Clay to the ranch an' git his wound fixed up an' you head back here with the rest of the outfit.'

Red nodded and the two men kicked their horses into a gallop along the trail towards Santa Rosa.

Warren watched them for a moment before turning to Mason. 'You go round the other side of the Mesa; I'll stay here. If we keep them penned up there until my cowboys arrive they won't have a chance to get away.

If McCoy or any of them comes down fire twice.'

Mason nodded his agreement and turned his horse to ride close to the jagged cliff-like wall of the Mesa.

Warren watched Mason ride away before pulling his horse slowly round. He rode to a group of rocks where he dismounted and made himself comfortable in a position from which he could see the trail from the Mesa.

On top of Pintada the three friends, refreshed by their meal, soon packed their belongings.

'When do we leave?' asked Abbe anxiously.

'It would be better to wait until the light begins to fade,' replied Mark, 'but if my hunch is right and Warren sends for his riders we may hev to move sooner; we must be away from here before they arrive. Frank, we'd better watch the trail from Santa Rosa.'

Frank nodded. 'Abbe, get some rest; we may hev a rough ride ahead of us. C'm on, Mark, we'll keep a look out.'

The two men hurried to the edge of the Mesa and lay flat watching the trail from town. A thin dust cloud rose some distance away.

'Look,' said Mark pointing in its direction. 'Two riders headin' for town.'

Frank's eyes narrowed as he looked at the sky. 'We've got some time in hand, it could be dark before Warren's outfit get here.'

The two men settled down to wait. The sun beat down unmercifully and except for the tell-tale dust cloud nothing moved in the parched countryside around them.

Frank must have dozed for suddenly he was startled by Mark who shook him vigorously.

'Time we went,' said Mark. 'Look, over there.' He pointed in the direction of Santa Rosa and Frank was startled to see a cloud of dust which indicated many riders heading towards Pintada Mesa.

'C'm on,' called Frank. 'Let's go.'

They scrambled away from the edge of the Mesa so that watching eyes below could not see their movements and jumping to their feet hurried to Abbe who, seeing them coming, got up quickly and untethered the horses.

They grabbed the reins and led the animals hastily across the Mesa. Before reaching the far side Mark turned into a cleft which ran downwards. He led the way slowly and carefully fearing that some slip on the smooth stones would bring disaster. The path fell gradually between two walls of rock until it opened out onto a wider trail. They were able to quicken the pace and were thankful when they reached the bottom.

'Wait here a moment,' said Mark and Frank and Abbe held the horses in check whilst the young deputy hurried to a cleft in the rock face.

He moved cautiously forward and shielding his eyes against the lowering sun carefully examined the ground which lay before him. No one was in sight and nothing disturbed the stillness. He waved to his two friends to follow him.

They slipped round the Mesa wall and over the shoulder of a hill before turning away from the huge rock. They pushed their horses forward faster keeping below the top of the ridge which afforded them some measure of cover.

Abbe, who kept glancing anxiously behind her, suddenly shouted a warning. Both Frank and Mark turned to see a lone rider a short distance behind them on the rim of the ridge.

'Mason!' yelled Frank and urged his horse faster.

The hired gunslinger spotted the three

riders and kicked his horse viciously in pursuit. As the animal stretched itself in full gallop Mason drew his Colt and fired twice.

The shots reverberated round the Mesa and shook Jake Warren out of his dreams of power. He jumped to his feet, raced to his horse and leaped into the saddle putting the animal into a fast gallop in the direction of the shots. He cut across the ground close to the wall of the Mesa. As he rounded the cliff-like face of rock he saw a dust cloud swirling above the edge of the ridge.

He knew that Mason must have spotted McCoy and his friends and he cursed that Red had not returned with the rest of his side-kicks before now. Warren pulled his horse round in an arc to try to cut across the ridge ahead of the three riders. As he turned he saw a group of horsemen riding at a fast pace from the direction of Santa Rosa.

Warren yelled triumphantly and drawing his Colt fired into the air to attract the attention of his men. An answering shot came back and Warren saw the riders change direction in their endeavour to put themselves ahead of the pursued.

The earth shook with pounding hoofs as Red brought his twelve riders close to the ridge alongside Warren.

'Good work, Red,' yelled Warren as they flew across the ground beside each other. 'We've got 'em!' The rancher nodded towards the dust cloud which lay a short way behind them below the ridge.

As they neared the edge the riders slowed up.

'We'll go across their path,' shouted Warren and put his horse over the hillside.

As the horsemen appeared Frank gasped with surprise and checked his horse. Abbe's cry drew Mark's attention away from Mason who had gained little in the pursuit.

Mark sized the situation in a flash. He knew they could not outrun Warren and his posse in a straight dash ahead. The rancher would easily cut across their path. 'This way,' yelled Mark and pulled his horse hard to the right.

Frank and Abbe hauled their mounts round in a dust-raising turn close behind Mark who was heading for some rough country about two miles away. He knew it would be hard for horses but he realised it was their only chance of evading their pursuers. The light was fading fast and he hoped that they would be able to hide in the labyrinth of gullies and ravines which cut the countryside ahead.

Seeing them turn Mason wheeled his horse at the same time to cut across the parched ground and shorten the distance between. Warren and his riders kept their horses at a full gallop down the slope and thundered on to flat country their horses at full stretch. Mason hit the trail behind the three riders slightly ahead of Warren and as the rancher gradually drew alongside the hired gunman drew his Colt to send lead flying after McCoy and his rescuers.

The three friends flattened themselves on their horses' backs as bullets whined over their heads. Frank realised that the extra burden of food and blankets which Mark and Abbe had brought along was telling on their mounts and that Warren and his outfit were gradually overhauling them. Desperately he pulled at his Colt and loosed off three shots at their pursuers. Frank and Mark dropped behind Abbe to give her more protection as they raced across the ground.

The posse continued to fill the air with lead in their effort to stop the riders ahead. Suddenly Mark jerked in the saddle with a yell of pain and Frank saw Mark's left arm go limp. He drew his horse closer to the deputy holding out his arm to assist him but

Mark shook his head indicating he could manage.

Abbe called to her horse for more effort but the sweating animal was already at full stretch. She had seen the rough ground ahead and it seemed as if they would never reach it but suddenly it was flashing under their hoofs. Desperately she looked round at Mark for some indication as to which direction she should take. She saw the deputy drawing alongside her and was shaken when she saw the blood streaming from the wound high up his arm.

Mark moved ahead and unhesitatingly pushed the animal down the steep side of a gully which cut across their path. His two friends followed suit and stones and earth flew as the three horses slid down the slope, thundered across the gully and pounded up the other side.

Light had vanished from the sky and the darkness coupled with the rough terrain made the ride dangerous. Two of Warren's riders lost their footing on the edge of the gully and plunged to the bottom amidst rolling horseflesh but the rancher yelled to the others to keep up the pace.

Once up the other side of the gully Mark turned slightly to the right and Frank found himself dropping down a steady slope into a ravine. Suddenly Mark pulled up sharp and indicated to the others to keep quiet.

Hoofs beat a loud tattoo on the hard ground above the head of the ravine and the three friends held their breath as they waited anxiously to hear if the riders turned to follow them. The pounding grew louder but it moved across the slope behind them and away to their left.

'Thought we might give them the slip in the darkness,' panted Mark.

'Good work,' returned Frank.

'You must have that wound attended to,' said Abbe urgently.

'We must get out of here before they find we have given them the slip,' replied Mark wiping the sweat from his forehead. 'I'll be all right,' he reassured Abbe as protestations sprang to her lips.

He turned his horse led the way back out of the ravine and turned in the same direction as Warren and his men.

'Mark, Warren and his men went this way,' said Abbe, alarm showing in her voice.

'It's all right,' Frank reassured her. 'Our tracks will be hidden in theirs. We'll turn off at some convenient point: Warren will soon realise we are no longer in front of him.'

Abbe nodded and rode close to Frank as they followed Mark silently. The deputy led the way carefully and after keeping amongst the posse's tracks for three hundred yards he swung to the left into a narrow cutting which dropped gently in front of them. As they moved downwards it became more difficult to see but Mark did not hesitate.

The hillside on their right sloped gently away in front of them forming the head of a gully which cut to their left. The path they were following moved around the hillside on their left which formed one side of the gully.

As they turned round the hillside Mark pulled his horse to a halt.

'We should be all right here,' he whispered indicating a small cave.

Before Frank could assist him Mark slipped from the saddle and as his feet touched the ground his knees buckled under him as he fainted with the loss of blood from the wound which had been aggravated by the hard ride.

Abbe stifled a cry of alarm and swung quickly out of the saddle. Frank leaped to his friend's side, dropped on one knee beside him and gently raised his head.

'Abbe, the canteen quick,' instructed Frank.

The girl quickly unfastened the canteen of water from the saddle and passed it to Frank who forced some of the liquid between his deputy's lips and splashed some over his hot face. Mark shuddered and blinked his eyes. He struggled to sit up but Frank held him back.

'Lie quiet a moment,' advised Frank, 'then we'll get you into the cave and see to thet arm.'

'Sorry,' muttered Mark. He grinned weakly at Abbe.

'You did well to last as long as you did an' you've certainly given Warren the slip,' replied Frank.

'I'd better try and fix up that arm,' said Abbe. 'Think you can get him into the cave, Frank?'

The sheriff helped Mark to his feet and supported him as they shuffled forward to the cave. Abbe hastily gathered some blankets from the horses and soon they had Mark comfortable under cover.

Whilst Abbe bathed and dressed the wound Frank unsaddled the horses and secured them for the night. He carried their belongings to the cave and made preparations for their stay. As he was carrying the last pack he suddenly froze in his tracks. The clop of horses on the hill above them grew louder as they moved along the hillside. He guessed there were two riders and as the noise of the hoofs came nearer he thought the riders had missed their way in the dark and were going to ride straight over the edge of the hill.

Frank heard a movement inside the cave and realised that Abbe was coming towards him. If she called out before she reached him the two men overhead would hear her. Swiftly but silently Frank placed his pack on the ground. As Abbe reached him she parted her lips to speak but Frank clamped his hand over her mouth stifling the words before they were uttered. Her eyes widened with amazement and alarm.

'Two men just above us,' Frank whispered in her ear.

He felt Abbe stiffen in his arms.

'It's all right,' Frank hastened to reassure her. 'They can't see us for the overhanging rocks.'

The horses stopped. 'C'm on let's git back to the camp,' said a raucous voice above them. 'It's useless searching in the dark.'

Frank and Abbe heard the horses turn and they waited until the sound of the hoofs faded in the distance. The girl breathed a sigh of relief and when Frank picked up the pack they hurried into the cave.

'How is he?' asked Frank nodding at Mark.

'He's sleeping now and feels weak with the loss of blood,' answered Abbe. 'The bullet's gone deep; he should see a doctor,' she added; her voice full of concern as a worried, compassionate look crossed her face.

'There's little we can do until daylight,' replied Frank. 'Will he be all right until then?'

Abbe frowned looking at Mark. 'I don't know,' she said. 'He was delirious when I was dressing his arm.' She turned to Frank. 'He should have a doctor really.'

The urgent note in Abbe's voice made up Frank's mind for him. He went over to his saddle and picked it up. Alarm crossed Abbe's face; her eyes widened as she realized the significance of the sheriff's action.

'Frank, you can't go to-night,' she pleaded. 'This is rough country which you don't know and Warren and his men are out there.'

'I must go,' replied Frank. 'Mark saved me and the least I can do is to get a doctor to him. You'll be all right here, Abbe, no one will find this cave in the dark and I'll be back before morning.'

'I'm not afraid for myself,' Abbe reassured him. 'It's you I'm worried about.'

Frank smiled and kissed her lightly. 'There's nothing to worry about; I'll go out of this rough country the same way as we came in.'

'But Warren?' cut in Abbe.

'I'll give him the slip in the dark,' replied Frank realising that it may not be as easy as it sounded.

The sheriff hurried to his horse and soon had it ready for the journey. He returned to the cave where Abbe sat beside the sleeping Mark. Bending down Frank took Abbe's hands in his and pulled her gently to her feet. His clear blue eyes looked down at her silently speaking of the love he felt for her. Their lips met in a long parting kiss. Abbe clung to him until Frank pushed her firmly but gently away. There were tears in her eyes as Frank turned to go.

'Be careful darling,' she whispered.

The sheriff smiled reassuringly. 'I'll be all right,' he replied. Frank hurried to his horse and led it slowly away from the cave.

Abbe watched him disappear into the darkness, a silent prayer on her lips.

Chapter Seven

Frank moved cautiously along the path into the gully and worked his way slowly upwards to the top of the hill. He paused, his eyes straining to find some sign of Warren's whereabouts. Satisfied that the camp was not close at hand he mounted his horse and rode steadily along the trail.

After riding for a quarter of a mile he pulled his horse to a halt when he saw the faint glow of a small camp fire ahead of him. He slipped from the saddle and after securing his horse he crept stealthily forward. The flicking light revealed the sleeping forms of several men and Frank thanked his good fortune that there was only one guard and he was huddled drowsily over the fire.

The sheriff slipped silently away. Warren was camped across the trail and as he made his way back to his horse Frank searched for some way round the encampment. Suddenly he realised Warren's shrewdness in picking this place to camp – the land on either side the trail fell precipitously into two ravines.

Dismayed, Frank had almost reached his horse when he noticed a break on the edge of the trail. He hurried forward and saw that a narrow path ran downwards but in the darkness he could not see how far or in which direction it went. He paused for only a brief moment and having made his decision, quickly released his horse. He led it forward to the path and when the animal hesitated he encouraged it with soft words. Frank moved warily along the path. On his right the shadow of the hillside cast a darkness across the void below whilst on his left the precipitous cliff face rose to the trail. The path moved downwards and Frank was fully aware of the terror in the animal he was leading. He spoke softly to it and led it firmly and but gently onwards. One false step could throw them into the ravine. Frank breathed a little easier when the path levelled out but still he kept to the same cautious pace. He realised that he must now be extra attentive not to make a sound as he estimated he must be passing Warren's camp. He froze as a flutter of stones were kicked by the horse's hoofs into the ravine but as all seemed quiet above he moved forward inch by inch. The neigh of a horse somewhere above him split the night air and froze Frank in his tracks. He clamped his hand over his horse's nostrils and whispered softly in its ear. The five minutes he stood there seemed like eternity to the sheriff but satisfied that the camp had not stirred he continued to feel his way steadily along the cliff face.

About a hundred yards further on the path started to rise slightly and Frank hoped that luck was with him. Suddenly it steepened in a series of steps and it was only with the utmost difficulty that Frank persuaded the animal to follow him. Once the roughness had been crossed the path widened and rose steadily to the trail above. As he climbed upwards Frank peered cautiously over the edge of the rock face and saw that Warren's camp lay about a quarter of a mile behind him. He thanked his good fortune as he reached the trail and climbed into the saddle.

The urge to ride fast was great but still exercising the utmost caution Frank rode at a walking pace knowing that the sound of galloping hoofs would rouse the camp. Once he was satisfied that he was far enough away he put the animal into a steady lope.

When he left the rough terrain he turned towards Pintada Mesa silhouetted against the starry sky and put his horse into a fast gallop. The night air whistled in Frank's ears as the animal stretched itself across the ground and he pulled his woollen coat closer around him as the coldness penetrated to his bones.

Frank kept his mount at a fast gallop until the houses of Santa Rosa loomed in the darkness. He slowed to a trot, eased himself in the saddle and reassuringly checked his gun in its holster. He pulled his sombrero further down on his forehead as he entered Santa Rosa by a back street. Keeping to the shadows he walked his horse slowly through the alleys and back streets, his eyes always on the alert for some movement but at this time of night all was quiet. The sheriff took a twisting rout across the town until he reached the back of Doctor Wilson's home which faced on to Main Street.

Frank froze in the saddle when he heard two horses moving along the street but as their hoof beats faded in the distance he swung down from his horse, tied it to a post and hurried to the house which was in darkness. Not wanting to wake the neighbours or attract outside attention he tapped lightly on the door. He waited impatiently but no one came. Frank crept cautiously round the house, peered anxiously up and down the street and seeing no one about picked up a handful of pebbles and threw them at the bedroom window. It seemed like eternity to the sheriff before the window was pushed open and Doctor Wilson's head appeared.

'Who the devil is down there?' growled the Doctor annoyed that his sleep had been disturbed in this unorthodox way.

'Quiet, Doc,' whispered Frank fearful that someone might hear them. 'Come down, it's a matter of life or death.'

Doc Wilson grunted but there was something in the urgency of the unknown man's voice which compelled him not to ask further questions from the window. He pulled the window down and Frank crossed to the porch where he stood with his back to the door anxiously watching the road.

A few minutes later Frank heard footsteps crossing the hall and he turned to see the doctor, holding a lamp, open the door. His eyes narrowed piercing the shadows to see who had disturbed his sleep. He held the light high to throw the beam across the sheriff's face. His eyes widened with surprise.

'McCoy!' he gasped. 'What the devil are you doing here?'

Frank pushed the doctor firmly but gently backwards and stepped quickly into the hall shutting the door behind him.

'See here, McCoy...' The protestation which sprang to the lips of the astonished, wide-eyed doctor was cut short by the sheriff.

'Sorry, Doc,' he apologised, 'but it's very urgent. Mark Stevens is wounded, way out in Pintada Flats; he's lost a lot of blood and needs attention.'

'I can't come out there at this time of night,' mumbled Wilson.

Frank stared incredulously at the small, grey-haired man standing in front of him. His hair was dishevelled and the collarless, unbuttoned shirt had been hastily stuffed into the top of his black trousers. A pair of worn carpet slippers slopped on his feet as he shuffled across the hall and put the lamp on a table.

Frank stepped quickly forward and grasped the older man by the shoulders.

'Doc,' he said pleadingly. 'You've got to come. Mark maybe dying.'

The doctor pulled himself away from Frank's grip as if he didn't want to face the sheriff's gaze.

'I can't,' he muttered.

'Can't!' Frank raised his voice in unbelief. 'You can't refuse to help a wounded man – what about your professional oath?'

The older man drew a sharp breath at this reminder. He slumped onto a chair holding his head in his hands. 'Don't ask me again McCoy, just get out of here and I'll forget you've ever been.'

Frank stared at the doctor hardly able to believe his ears. This was not the Doc Wilson who was loved and respected in Santa Rosa; this was not the man who had come west with Mal Clements and had helped to build the town.

'Doc,' snapped Frank, 'what's gotten into you? I am asking you again an' if necessary I'll take you at the point of a gun.' To emphasize his words he pulled his Colt from his holster tilting the muzzle under the doctor's nose.

Wilson straightened on the chair. He looked at Frank his eyes full of regret. 'Frank,' he whispered, 'don't force me to come. I can't work against the law.'

'The law!' Frank gasped. 'There's no law in this town at the moment. Warren's trying to run the law – framing me, putting those two gun slingers in...' The sheriff stopped, staring incredulously at the dejected figure in front of him as a thought suddenly pounded in his brain. 'Warren!' he hissed. 'You mean you can't work against Warren! What's he got on you, Doc?'

The doctor looked pleadingly at Frank. 'Leave me alone, please. If he got to know I'd helped you...' He left the sentence unfinished knowing full well that Frank knew the rest.

'He need never know,' replied the sheriff, 'if that will ease your mind, but I did think you were one man I could trust. You don't think I killed Clements, do you?'

'I don't know what to think,' answered the doctor. 'Things looked pretty black for you...'

'I know,' cut in Frank, 'but I was framed an' I reckon by Warren. Look, Doc, I wanted to clean this town of Warren an' his bunch before he got a tight hold of it. I was in his way so he planted this killin' on me and through it set himself up as an upholder of the law. I still aim to clean him up an' I thought you would be one to see it my way. It's not too late, Doc; put yourself right again, this town needs men like you.'

'It's no good, Frank,' mumbled Wilson wearily.

Frank grunted disgustedly, slipped his Colt back into its holster, swung on his heel and strode to the door. His hand was on the knob when the doctor spoke again.

'Wait,' he called.

Frank spun round, a hopeful light in his eyes. He looked questioningly at the doctor who did not speak for a moment. The sheriff knew a battle was going on inside the mind of the man sitting in front of him. Slowly, Wilson got to his feet. He looked at Frank.

'I'll come,' he whispered. 'Just wait until I get ready.'

'Good man, Doc,' approved Frank enthusiastically, a smile parting his lips.

The grey haired man shuffled to the stairs and climbed them slowly as if the problem still weighed heavily on his shoulders. Half way up he paused and half turned as if to retrace his steps. His fingers twitched nervously on the rail; his mouth moved, silently arguing the matter to himself; his eyes stared vacantly into the hall.

The sheriff watched him anxiously, wondering how long this man had been putting on a front every time he appeared in public.

The doctor's eyes slowly focused on Frank and the sight of the sheriff brought the doctor back to reality. A shudder ran through his body. Slowly the old man turned and climbed the stairs.

A quarter of an hour passed before the doctor reappeared. Frank smiled when he saw the change in the man who walked briskly down the stairs. His hair was brushed neatly back from his forehead; he had changed his trousers for a pair which were neatly creased; his black frock-coat hung smartly from his shoulders and a black necktie was carefully tied at the neck of a clean white shirt. He carried his bag and a flat wide-brimmed sombrero.

He stopped in front of Frank. 'Thanks,' he said, 'for making me see the right thing to do.' He straightened himself pulling his shoulders back; his eyes gleamed with a new hope; he held his head erect his chin jutting with a new found confidence.

He blew out the light and Frank, keeping close to the doctor followed him to the back door and across the small yard to the stable. The sheriff saddled a horse quickly and as they led it outside he glanced anxiously at the sky.

'It's goin' to be light before we reach Mark,' said Frank. 'Warren and his bunch are camped across the only way in that I know.'

A look of fear flashed across Wilson's face but it was gone almost before Frank noticed it. 'Don't worry,' he said. 'I know that country. Give me an idea where Mark is and I'll find a way round Warren.'

Frank quickly traced a rough map, in the dust outside the stable and explained the position of the cave.

When Frank had finished the doctor grunted. 'Good,' he said. 'I know another way in, it will take a bit longer but will keep us away from Warren. Come on let's get as far as possible before daybreak.'

Frank erased the map with his boot before hurrying to his horse. They rode steadily through the town and once they reached the outskirts they put their horses into a fast gallop through grassland and into the desert.

As they neared Pintada Mesa the faint streaks of light were marking the eastern sky with a new day. Doc Wilson led the way close to the cliff-like walls of Pintada, across the shoulder of the hill which abutted the Mesa and rode straight across into Pintada Flats well to the north of the section in which Frank had left Abbe and Mark.

Light was flooding the countryside of New Mexico as the Doctor led the way into a gully which they followed for four miles before swinging to the left and climbing onto a ridge. They rode along the ridge just below the skyline for two miles before turning over the top into another gully which headed due south. The two men kept a steady pace until the gully narrowed and their way was barred by a steep hillside. Wilson pulled his horse to a standstill.

'Where do we go from here?' asked Frank looking around for some way out of the gully.

Wilson nodded to the hillside in front of them. 'We're not far from the cave, but we've got to get to the top of there,' he said. 'There's a narrow path but once we are on the top we've got to ride along that ridge.' He indicated the land running away to the right. 'There's a sheer drop on either side and I'm afraid we will be silhouetted against the sky. We'll be in danger of being seen but that's a chance we've got to take.'

Frank nodded. 'Let's go,' he said curtly.

Doc Wilson led the way along the narrow path which twisted and turned up the hillside. It was a strenuous climb and both men and horses were breathing heavily as they moved onto the ridge. Frank surveyed the land quickly. The doctor turned his horse along the ridge encouraging the animal with quiet orders. One false step would send both man and horse hurtling down the steep slopes. They had gone about a quarter of a mile when the doctor stopped. He turned in the saddle and without a word to Frank pointed to a ravine along which three cowboys were riding slowly.

'Good job they were riding away from us,' said Frank as the three men moved round a bend.

The doctor nodded. 'C'm on, let's get off here as soon as possible,' he said kicking his horse forward.

Another half mile took them to the end of the ridge where the narrow trail wound down the hillside into a gully. They had not gone far when the pound of horses' hoofs on the hilltop made Frank glance anxiously round for some cover.

'Over there,' he called softly to the doctor turning his horse towards a ledge of overhanging rock.

The two men rode swiftly towards the cover and reached it with the sound of galloping horses growing louder. Frank and the doctor slipped from the saddles and stood beside their animals soothing them lest some movement should disclose their position. They heard the horses slow down and finally stop at the edge of the gully above them.

'No one in this gully, boss,' said a gruff voice.

'They could be anywhere,' came the reply. Frank looked sharply at the doctor as he recognised Jake Warren's voice. 'But with one of them wounded they're more than likely holed up somewhere.' He paused for a moment as if gathering his thoughts. 'Red, we'll call everyone in; detail three men to keep patrolling the Flats and the rest of us will pull out, there's important things to see to in Santa Rosa.'

Red acknowledged the orders and the two men turned their horses and rode away. Frank and Doc Wilson waited until the hoof beats faded in the distance before they climbed into the saddles. The doctor quickened the pace along the gully which twisted and turned until it broke into another gully along which the two men rode for a quarter of a mile before the doctor stopped.

He pointed to the hillside on the right. 'Is that the cave?' he asked.

Frank studied the landscape carefully. 'That's it,' he replied excitedly.

They urged their horses quickly to the path and were soon following it towards the cave. The clop of the horses' hoofs brought Abbe hurrying to the entrance to the cave. She raised her rifle and peered cautiously round the rocks, but breathed a sigh of relief when she saw Frank and Doc Wilson. Springing to her feet she ran to meet them.

'Abbe Clements!' said the doctor in amazement as they pulled their horses to a stop. He glanced sharply at Frank. 'You didn't tell me...' He turned to Abbe. 'Miss Clements, what are you doing here?'

Abbe smiled at the doctor as the two men swung down from the saddles. 'I'm engaged to Frank, remember?' she replied. 'I believe his story and he thought I was in danger from Warren so here I am.'

'This is no place for a woman,' said the doctor coolly.

'Any better suggestions?' snapped Frank.

'We'll think of one,' answered Wilson, 'but let me see Mark now.'

'How is he?' asked Frank as Abbe led the way to the cave.

'He's had a fairly comfortable night and there's been no more bleeding but he's very weak,' replied the girl.

The doctor was soon on his knees beside Mark and quickly but gently removed the bandages. He did not speak until he had examined the wound carefully.

'You've done very well, Abbe,' he complimented. 'Please boil some more water.'

The girl hurried to the back of the cave

where a can containing water was already on the fire.

The doctor looked at Mark who grinned faintly. 'Is it goin' to be all right, doc?' he whispered.

'Sure, son,' Wilson replied quietly, 'but I've got to get that lead out and that will hurt some.'

'Anything you say, doc,' gasped Mark. 'Just get me right to help Frank fight Warren.'

The doctor opened the wound and probed for the bullet. Gently he inserted the instrument deeper feeling for the lead. The cowboy winced with pain and Frank held his arms tightly. Mark bit hard on the cork which the doctor had put between his teeth; sweat started to pour from his forehead; his whole body seemed to be on fire. Still the doctor could not feel the bullet and he probed deeper. Mark shuddered and suddenly relaxed.

'He's fainted,' whispered Frank.

'Good,' muttered Wilson.

Frank watched the grey-haired man skilfully search for the bullet. Suddenly he saw the firm but gentle hand tighten. Slowly the doctor pulled at the lead and carefully withdrew it from Mark's arm. Abbe had the water ready and the doctor quickly cleaned and dressed the wound. He did not speak until he had finished when with a sigh of relief and a grunt of satisfaction he straightened and climbed to his feet.

'Will he be all right?' asked Frank anxiously.

'Sure, he'll be all right, but he'll have to stay quiet for a few days,' replied Wilson.

Frank nodded. 'Thanks, doc,' he said. 'I'll stay with him but what about...'

He was interrupted by Abbe who stepped forward. 'Don't worry about me,' she said. 'I'll stay as well.'

The doctor looked hard at her. 'That's very noble of you young lady,' he said, 'but he won't be able to move out of here for four days and this is no place for you.'

'Doc's right, Abbe,' said Frank. 'You'd be better out of here, but where...'

'I'll take her back to Santa Rosa,' suggested the doctor. 'She can stay at my place and if she keeps out of sight Warren need never know.'

'A good idea,' approved Frank and turned to stop Abbe's protestations. 'I'd be happier,' he assured her, 'an' when Mark's fit to move we'll find some place an' contact you.'

The girl agreed and whilst they enjoyed some coffee they discussed the situation.

'Abbe can't come out with me now,' pointed out Wilson, 'it would be too risky with Warren's men combing the Flats. I've got to go back to town but I'll return tonight and take Abbe out in the dark.'

He said goodbye, climbed into the saddle and followed the path round the side of the hill into the gully which led on the trail out of Pintada Flats. He had been riding on the trail for about a hundred yards when he heard hoof beats behind him. He turned in the saddle. Jake Warren and Ed Mason were overtaking him at a fast clip!

Chapter Eight

Doc Wilson controlled the urge to put his horse into a gallop when he saw Warren. He realised that he must keep calm and outwardly he must show no sign of the real reason he was in Pintada Flats.

The two horses pounded up to the doctor and as he pulled up alongside Wilson, Jake Warren greeted him. 'Hi, doc! What are you doin' way out here at this time of day?' he called.

The doctor adjusted his sombrero as he glanced at the two men. 'Just been out for an early morning ride,' he said. 'I like to come out here to see the sun rise.'

Warren's eyes narrowed and he looked at the doctor suspiciously. 'Seems a strange part of the country to pick,' he commented.

'Then you haven't an eye for the beauties of the early morning,' replied Wilson. 'You must come with me one morning and I'll show you the way the sun plays in and out of those gullies and ravines, besides, the early ride is refreshing before a day amongst the sick.'

'Guess so,' muttered Warren. 'But why the bag?' he asked indicating the small black bag hanging from the saddle.

'I always carry that,' answered the doctor. 'You never know when you may want it.'

'Did you need it this morning?' quizzed Warren watching the older man closely.

The doctor's face remained impassive. He shook his head. 'Haven't seen a soul,' he said quietly.

'An' where you headin' now?' asked the rancher.

'Santa Rosa,' replied Wilson. 'I've my morning rounds to do, but I might ask what you are doin' out here?'

Warren grunted. 'McCoy broke out of jail, helped by Mark Stevens and Miss Clements. We followed them into the Flats but lost them in the dark. You sure you ain't seen them?'

Doc Wilson shook his head. 'Like I said I haven't seen a soul.'

'Wal, if you do, let me know at once,' said Warren curtly. 'C'm on, Ed.' He kicked his horse forward followed by Mason.

The doctor watched them ride away leaving a cloud of dust rising behind them. He smiled grimly to himself and put his horse into a trot towards Santa Rosa.

As he went on his rounds his mind was preoccupied with the predicament of the three friends in Pintada Flats. During the afternoon he was passing The Ace of Spades when Warren swung through the doors on to the sidewalk accompanied by Ed Mason and Clay Duncan.

'Hello there,' greeted Warren heartily. 'C'm on in an' hev a drink, The Ace of Spades is open again.'

Doc Wilson glanced sharply at the three men and anger swelled inside him when he noticed the tin stars pinned to the shirts of the gun-slingers. He clenched his hands tightly as he controlled his temper and his tongue.

'You re-opened mighty soon after Clements' death,' he said quietly.

'Wal, the law here figured it best,' grinned Warren indicating his two companions. 'They reckoned there might be trouble if we kept it shut too long.'

'An' what's happening to the money?' asked the doctor eyeing Warren coldly.

'Don't worry about thet, Doc,' laughed Warren clapping his hand on Wilson's shoulder. 'It's all being banked for Miss Clements for when we find her. C'm on now hev that drink.'

The doctor grunted and scowled at Warren shaking his hand roughly from his shoulder. 'I daren't touch a drink, an' you know it,' he snarled.

Warren's face darkened and the two gun-slingers tensed themselves.

'You should accept Mister Warren's hospitality,' snapped Mason reaching forward to grab the lapels of the doctor's coat.

'Let him go,' intervened Warren. 'He's only a small time doctor, good fer nothin' else an' as long as he sticks to doctoring it's all right by me.' He looked shrewdly at the older man. 'And better fer himself,' he added quietly.

The threat in the words was not lost on Wilson who swung on his heels and left the three men. Warren watched him through narrow eyes. He stroked his chin thought-fully and suddenly crossed to the door of the Ace of Spades. He pushed it open and stepped inside.

'Red!' he shouted and in response to the call his foreman turned from the bar and hurried to him. 'Put Roy Manners on to trail Doc Wilson an' report anything un-usual.'

'Right, boss,' acknowledged Red who returned to the bar and spoke quickly to one of the cowboys.

Warren rejoined the hired guns and the three men hurried along the sidewalk to the sheriff's office, whilst Roy Manners swung out of the saloon and strolled casually in the direction of Doc Wilson's home.

The doctor spent an uneasy afternoon turning the recent events over in his mind. From personal experience he knew Warren to be a blackmailer, a man who would use unsavoury knowledge to hold a man in his power and force him to betray the trust of his patients so that he could use that knowledge to his own advantage.

Many of Mal Clements' secrets had reached Warren through him and although he knew that Warren's threats were not idle ones he saw a chance to put himself right with his own conscience by helping Abigail Clements and Frank McCoy.

Wilson waited impatiently for night unaware that a cowboy amused himself whittling at a piece of wood whilst watching the house.

The light was beginning to fade from the sky when the doctor collected his black bag and left the house by the back door. As he hurried across the yard to the stable a cowboy rose to his feet, crossed the main street and keeping to the shadows kept the stable under observation. Wilson saddled his horse, swung into the saddle and turned into the back street.

Roy Manners watched him go before hurrying along Main Street to his horse still tied to the hitching rail outside of The Ace of Spades. He rode up an alley towards the street along which Doc Wilson was riding. He rode cautiously round the corner and saw the doctor was already at the end of the street leaving town. Manners smiled to himself as he settled in the saddle – this was going to be too easy.

The doctor kept a steady pace through the grasslands but quickened it when he reached the desert. The sun had sunk beyond the horizon, leaving a faint glow in the west and with its going a chill wind played across the sand. The rider pulled his coat tighter around him, hunched himself in the saddle and tried to reassure himself that all would be well.

Pintada Mesa rose high and black against the night sky. It stood like some ominous sentinel watching every movement across the countryside. The doctor shivered and as he rode over the shoulder of the hill close to the Mesa he glanced behind him. Suddenly, he had an uneasy feeling that someone was watching him. He pulled his horse to a halt and straining his eyes searched the dark countryside behind him. He could see no movement and grunting disgustedly to himself he glanced up at the huge cliffs towering above him.

'Guess you'd send a shiver through anybody at this time of night,' he muttered and pulling his horsed round he sent it down the slope at a brisk trot towards Pintada Flats.

Only the horse's hoofs and the swish of the wind broke the stillness, but the doctor still felt a little uneasy. He turned in the saddle and glanced over his shoulder. A tenseness ran through his body when he saw the outline of a rider break the skyline and slip quickly over the shoulder of the hill in his direction. The doctor's brain pounded as his thoughts tumbled through all the possibilities of the shadow on his trail. He realised Warren must have been suspicious when he met him in the Flats and had had him watched. Wilson was tempted to turn his horse and head for Santa Rosa but he controlled the urge when he thought of his chance to make peace with himself.

The doctor quickened the pace hoping to throw off his pursuer but the man behind closed the gap between them knowing that he would have to keep close to the doctor once they reached the Flats. Wilson twisted and turned through ravines and gullies but before long he realised there was a skilful man on his trail. He quickened the pace in one last attempt to lose his follower. If this failed, he knew there was only one thing he could do!

The cowboy stayed close to the doctor and as Wilson turned into a narrow ravine he swung from the saddle and sent his horse into a cut in the hill face. He drew his Colt from his holster and scrambled on to a rock. The clop of hoofs grew nearer and a rider emerged slowly out of the blackness. As the man passed close to him the doctor leaped from the rock crashing his Colt hard on the man's head and hurling him from the saddle. Both men crashed to the ground. The doctor rolled over, his breath driven from his body. He scrambled quickly to his feet and with his gun held ready he moved slowly towards the silent figure. Panting hard, the doctor stared at the man on the ground. He dropped on one knee beside the cowboy and realising that he was dead rose slowly to his feet relieved that he would not have to shoot a man in cold blood.

The doctor recovered his sombrero, quickly mounted his horse and sent the animal forward along the ravine. It was not long before he neared the cave and the clop of the hoofs on the rock brought Frank hurrying to see who approached.

'Who's there?' he called softly.

'Doc Wilson,' came the reply as the doctor appeared out of the blackness.

'Thank goodness.' Relief showed in Frank's voice. 'We thought you weren't goin' to get here.'

The doctor swung wearily out of the saddle. 'Tell you in a moment. Have you any coffee?' said Wilson.

'Sure,' replied Frank as they entered the cave. 'What's happened?' he asked startled as the fire-light revealed the doctor's white face and dust-covered clothes.

Before the doctor answered the sheriff's question he turned to Mark and examined him carefully but quickly. 'How's he been?' he asked.

'Quiet, slept most of the time,' replied Abbe handing the doctor a mug of hot coffee.

'Good,' approved Wilson sitting down. He sipped his coffee and told his story.

Frank listened without comment until the doctor had finished. He frowned. 'This complicates matters,' he said. 'Warren must have been suspicious this morning when he saw you out here an' set thet man to trail you. When he finds out thet he's not back in town when you are he's goin' to wonder. You got to be careful, doc, especially with Abbe in town.'

'Would it be better if she didn't come back?' said Wilson anxiously.

'I'd rather she was away from here; there's no tellin' what might happen,' replied Frank.

The doctor nodded his agreement. 'We'd better get going,' he said as he got to his feet. 'Wrap up well, Abbe, it's cold across the desert to-night.'

Abbe was soon ready and Frank accompanied her to her horse which he had saddled for her. She paused with her hand on the saddle and turned to Frank.

'Be careful, darling,' she said softly.

Frank took her hand and drew her close to him. 'That goes for you too,' he whispered and leaning forward he kissed her longingly.

As they parted Frank turned to Wilson. 'Watch out fer Warren,' he warned.

'I'll be careful,' reassured the doctor, 'and don't worry about Abbe, I'll look after her.'

He swung into the saddle and Frank helped Abbe to mount her horse.

'We'll contact you as soon as Mark can travel,' he said. 'Be careful through the Flats.'

'Goodbye, Frank,' whispered Abbe, her voice betraying her real feelings as she sent the horse forward close behind Doc Wilson.

The sheriff watched them go but they were soon swallowed up by the darkness and only the clop of the hoofs came back to Frank to indicate their progress. As the sound faded Frank returned to his lonely vigil beside the wounded Mark in the cave in Pintada Flats.

Chapter Nine

Jake Warren strolled on to the long wooden verandah of the neat one-storeyed ranch house. He leaned against the rail and casually rolled himself a cigarette glancing every now and then across the lush grassland which stretched away from the house. Large herds of cattle grazed on the gently sloping ground and in the corrals to the right of the house several cowboys were breaking mustangs. Warren lit his cigarette slowly, drew deeply, and blew a long smoke cloud into the air.

As he looked around him a smile of satisfaction crossed his face. His ranch prospered and the recent events in Santa Rosa had gone his way. It wouldn't be long before the power he wanted would be his.

His thoughts were interrupted when the door behind him opened. He turned and leaned back on the rail. His smile broadened.

'Hello, Gloria.' He greeted the tall, slim, blonde girl who stepped from the house and crossed the boards towards him.

Her smile revealed rows of even white teeth and her blue eyes sparkled with contentment as she breathed deeply, enjoying the fresh morning air.

'What a beautiful morning,' she said. 'We must take a ride shortly.' She leaned forward on the rail beside Warren. Her eyes twinkled as she looked up at him. 'I trust you had a pleasant night,' she whispered.

Warren grinned and turned to lean on the rail beside her. Gloria Linden slipped her arm through his and Warren glanced admiringly at the girl beside him. Her silken blonde hair dropped to her shoulders framing an oval face. The tight flowered dress accentuated her slim, supple body. As he looked at her Warren realised she must inherit her beauty from her mother for she had little in common with her father, old Silas Linden, except that they both loved money. Silas, for the drink it would buy and Gloria for the power and security which went with it.

Warren's thoughts were interrupted as Gloria suddenly gripped his arm tightly and pointed across the grassland to a cloud of dust which was fast approaching the ranch-house. The rancher straightened himself and narrowed his eyes, straining to identify the rider.

'Looks like trouble the way this cowboy's raising the dust,' said Gloria.

Warren grunted and hurried into the ranch house to reappear a moment later with a spy glass. He trained it on the rider and quickly drew him into focus.

'It's Sam Baker!' he exclaimed excitedly. 'I left him in the Flats; reckon they must hev gotten on to McCoy!'

'Will this leave the way open?' asked Gloria eagerly.

'Sure will, if they've got McCoy an' Stevens,' answered Warren. 'Although, things have gone my way pretty well up to now.'

'They certainly have,' agreed Gloria. 'McCoy framed with the killing of Clements and you setting yourself as upholding the law.'

Warren laughed loudly. 'Yeah, I've got the town eating out of my hand an' two hired killers set up as lawmen. The Ace of Spades is pullin' the money in an' when Sam brings in news of Miss Clements I'll be able to move in as working in her interests.'

'Or settling the affairs of the late, lamented Abbe Clements,' finished off Gloria with a grin.

The rancher laughed. 'Sure, you catch on quick. And then for the Lazy A.'

The sound of the hard ridden horse brought Red Holliday hurrying from the corral where he had been supervising the breaking of the mustangs.

'Looks like some news from the Flats, boss,' he said tipping his hat to Gloria.

Warren nodded. Sam pulled his horse to a dust-raising, sliding halt, in front of them. The cowboy was out of the saddle before it had stopped and stood gasping for breath in front of Warren.

'We've found Roy Manners out in the Flats, dead!' he panted.

'What!' Warren gasped. He looked sharply at Red who stared incredulously at Baker. Horror crossed Gloria's face as she stared wide-eyed at the dust-covered cowboy.

'Reckon he'd been dead about a day when we found him,' confirmed Baker.

'Any signs of who did it?' asked Warren.

The cowboy shook his head. 'No, hoof marks went off in all directions, reckon Roy's horse obliterated the marks left by the killer,' replied Sam wearily.

'All right, Sam. You've had a hard ride, get yourself cleaned up and have a good meal,' said Warren. 'Then get yourself a fresh horse and return to the Flats. Keep thet patrol goin'.'

'Right, boss,' said Baker gratefully. He picked up his horse's reins and led the sweating animal to the stable.

Warren rubbed his chin thoughtfully as he turned to his foreman. 'Red, I've two theories about this killin',' he said, the words coming slowly and deliberately. 'I put Roy on to trail Doc Wilson; maybe he found somethin' out about the whereabouts of McCoy an' rode out to the Flats where he was jumped by McCoy, or else he followed the Doc who got wise to him and jumped him himself.'

'There's only one way to find out, boss,' suggested Red, 'an' thet's to pay Doc Wilson a visit.'

'Thet's jest what I figured,' answered Warren. 'Get the horses.'

The foreman hurried to the stable and the rancher turned to Gloria. 'Sorry, honey,' he apologised. 'We'll have to take thet ride later.'

Gloria moved close to Warren and ran her hands slowly up his chest and round his neck. 'Be careful, Jake,' she whispered and kissed him longingly on the lips.

As their lips parted slowly, Warren nodded. 'I'll be all right,' he said. 'We'll pick Mason an' Duncan up in town.' He drew Gloria's arms from around his neck and holding her hand, walked slowly towards the stable.

Red appeared with the two horses, the two men climbed into the saddles and with a curt wave to Gloria, Warren kicked his horse into a fast trot towards Santa Rosa.

Half an hour later they slipped from the saddles in front of the sheriff's office, leaped up the steps and in two strides were across the sidewalk and into the office.

Duncan and Mason looked up sharply as the door burst open. Warren quickly told them the news of the killing. 'Come on you two,' he concluded. 'We're goin' to pay Doc Wilson a visit an' maybe you can earn some more of your pay.'

The four men hurried from the office, past the false-fronted shops, to the row of houses at the end of Main Street. They swung through the white-painted gate and strode up the path to Doc Wilson's house. Warren rapped hard on the door but his knocking remained unanswered. He cursed furiously and turned to the three men waiting at the foot of the verandah.

'We'll split up and search the town for Wilson,' he ordered briskly. 'Red you stay here and watch the house; Duncan, you take one side of the street, Mason you the other.'

The four men hurried down the path little knowing that they had been observed by

Abigail Clements from an upstairs window.

Abbe had been in her room when she heard the gate squeak. She peered cautiously from behind lace curtains and was startled to see Jake Warren, accompanied by his foreman and two hired guns hurrying along the path towards the house.

Everything had gone well since they had left the lonely cave in Pintada Flats. The ride had been uneventful, and after a good sleep, the doctor had issued careful instructions regarding Abbe's stay.

'No one must see you,' he had told her, 'and when I'm out on my rounds on no account open the door to anyone, it doesn't matter who it is, trust no one until Frank contacts us again.'

Abbe had agreed, and whenever the doctor was out she locked all the doors and windows and retreated to the room upstairs which Doc Wilson had set aside for her, and from which she now saw Warren and his sidekicks approaching the house.

She waited anxiously, fearing the worst, but breathed a sigh of relief when she saw the four men hurry back down the path. She saw them pause against the gate where Warren appeared to be issuing orders. The four men split up and Abbe knew that all was far from well when Warren's foreman, Red Holliday, crossed the street and lounged against the railings of the house opposite keeping Doc Wilson's home under observation.

Warren accompanied Ed Mason whilst Clay Duncan worked the other side of the street. They moved slowly along Main Street, keeping a watchful eye on every building they passed; they enquired in the stores, at the café, the livery stables, the bank, the Wells Fargo office, and every other place which the doctor may have visited, but when they reached the end of Main Street, they were as near finding Doc Wilson as when they started.

'Guess, he must be out of town,' said Warren mopping his brow with a red handkerchief. 'Thet was thirsty work. C'm on we'll get ourselves a drink. Guess there's nothing we can do but wait until Red sees him return home.'

The three men hurried along the sidewalk to the Ace of Spades. Warren paused at the door.

'Clay, tell Red we'll be in here waiting news,' ordered Warren.

Duncan nodded and hurried down the street anxious to return for his drink.

The afternoon wore on and their glasses

had been refilled a number of times before Red Holliday hurried in with the news that Doc Wilson had returned home. They finished their drinks quickly and the four men hurried from the saloon.

When Doc Wilson opened the door of his house he was surprised to see Abbe, racing down the stairs to meet him.

'What's the matter?' asked the doctor as he dropped his bag and hat onto a chair.

Abbe grasped his arms. Fear touched her voice as she spoke. 'Jake Warren's been here this afternoon with his foreman and those two gunmen.'

Wilson looked alarmed, but his voice was calm. 'Steady, my dear, it may not be anything much...'

'It must be,' cried Abbe,' or why would he bring those men with him. Besides, I could see by his face that there was trouble for you. He left Red Holliday to watch the house and as soon as you returned Holliday hurried away.'

'All right, Abbe, maybe we'd better leave,' said the doctor. 'Get your things, hurry.'

Abbe ran upstairs and the doctor went through to the back room and was about to hurry to the stables when loud hammering at the front door halted him. He turned slowly and shrugged his shoulders wearily, knowing that now he would have to face Warren wondering how much the rancher knew.

The hammering continued and galvanised the doctor into action. He hurried to the stairs and climbed them quickly to meet Abbe who came from her room, a frightened look on her face.

'It's Warren!' she whispered, a tremor in her voice.

The doctor nodded. 'I know,' he replied. 'Abbe, keep out of sight; don't show yourself at all no matter what they do or what you hear said keep out of sight; don't let Warren see you, don't let him get his hands on you.'

He turned and hurried down the stairs to open the front door. Before he could speak he was pushed back into the hall and without any ceremony the four men stepped inside and slammed the door behind them.

'What's the meaning of this?' stormed the doctor. 'Bursting your way in here.'

Warren smiled but his eyes were cold, foreboding ill for the man in front of him. 'We just want a little chat,' he replied smoothly.

'Does it take four of you?' snapped Wilson.

'Thet depends on you,' answered Warren,

his grin widening as the doctor looked puzzled.

'If it depends on me, then the talkings finished,' answered the doctor testily. 'Good day, gentlemen.'

'Come, Doc, thet's no way to greet the new lawmen of Santa Rosa,' admonished Warren.

The three men behind him laughed as the doctor's face darkened.

'Lawmen!' he snapped. 'Hired guns hiding behind tin stars to try to give your crooked deals a front.'

Warren's smile vanished; his lips tightened and anger clouded his eyes. 'Careful what you say,' he snarled, 'or else thet little secret between you and I may be a secret no longer.' He paused a moment to let the implication of his words sink in 'You've played things my way up to now, see that it stays thet way.'

The doctor did not speak. Warren waited a moment and then pushed roughly passed him towards the door of the sitting room.

'We'll go in here for our chat,' he snapped.

Before Wilson realised what was happening Ed Mason pushed him unceremoniously through the door to send him sprawling across a chair. As he picked himself up he started to protest.

'Now see here,' he began, but his words were cut short when Clay Duncan grabbed the lapels of his coat and dumped him into a chair.

'Now listen to what Mister Warren has to say,' cautioned Duncan.

Warren stood in front of the doctor. He spoke slowly and deliberately. 'What were you doin' in Pintada Flats when I saw you the other morning?'

'I gave you my answer then,' replied Wilson.

'And I didn't much like it,' hissed Warren.

'It's up to you whether you believe it or not,' said the doctor.

Warren's eyes narrowed as he looked at the man in the chair. 'Where's Frank Mc-Coy?' he snapped suddenly.

Wilson stared at the rancher in surprise. 'McCoy? How should I know where he is?' he replied.

'They're somewhere in the Flats; you were in the Flats and I happen to know that either McCoy or Stevens is wounded,' said Warren, 'and it doesn't take much imagination to link these facts together.'

The startled doctor hid his feelings and did not speak.

'Have you been in Pintada Flats again since I saw you?' snapped Warren.

'No, why should I?' answered Wilson.

'Thought you liked riding there.'

'I do, but I don't go every day,' said the doctor calmly.

'Seen anything of Roy Manners lately?' snapped the rancher in his attempts to trap Wilson.'

A puzzled look crossed the doctor's face as if he couldn't follow Warren's train of questions.

'Roy Manners?' he said casually. 'Well, I believe I saw him around town – might have been yesterday.'

'Yesterday?' smirked Warren. 'You wouldn't because Manners was dead!'

'Dead!' gasped Doc Wilson. 'But I'm sure I saw him in town.'

'I think you saw him in Pintada Flats,' snarled Warren, 'and I think you know more about this than you care to say.'

'About what?' said Wilson a puzzled tone in his voice.

'About the killing; about McCoy and...' Warren's words were cut short as Wilson protested.

'I don't!' he cried.

Warren glanced at his two hired gunmen.

His nod was almost imperceptible as he spoke through tight lips. 'All right, you take over.'

They stepped forward and the doctor recoiled in his chair but there was no escaping the two broad, hairy hands which dragged him upright. A huge fist crashed into his face sending him sprawling across a table which overturned with a crash.

Warren stepped forward to where the doctor struggled to push himself up from the floor. 'Care to tell me anything, doc?' he asked smoothly.

The doctor wiped the blood from his mouth with the back of his hand and glared angrily at the dark-haired rancher.

'Warren, I've finished with your dirty ways now. This has finally convinced me,' he hissed, 'that I no longer play along with you. No, I daren't say anything about the filthy work I've done for you, you've no need to fear on that account, but I'll do no more for you.'

Warren stood over the doctor glaring down at him. 'All I want is some information from you,' he snarled.

'You've had all the information you're getting from me,' answered the doctor between tight lips as he struggled to his feet.

The two hired guns closed in on him and whilst Clay Duncan held the old man Ed Mason sank his fist into his stomach. The doctor groaned and doubled up when Duncan let go of him. Mason slapped the back of his hand across Wilson's face sending him staggering back against the wall. His knees started to buckle and he began to sink slowly to the floor but the powerful hands of Clay Duncan grabbed him once again and straightened him.

Mason's huge hand slapped quickly back and forth across the doctor's cheeks jerking his head from side to side. The pain screamed into the doctor's brain.

Warren laid an arresting hand on Mason's arm.

'Care to say anythin' doc?' drawled Warren.

The doctor shook his head and as he did so a hand crashed into his face again. He felt himself dragged forward and dumped into a chair, but he was no sooner seated than a fist pounded his face, sending him flying from the chair to crash into a heap against the wall.

'All right, boys, hold it,' ordered Warren as the two gunmen pulled the doctor to his feet. He hung limp in their arms and slumped in a heap when they dropped him into a chair.

'Find some water,' said the rancher turning to his foreman who hurried from the room to return a few moments later with a jug the contents of which he flung in the unconscious man's face.

The doctor shuddered and groaned from between his cut lips. The ugly bruises on his cheeks were swelling, his eyes were slowly closing, and the blood ran down from the cut above his left eye. He raised his hand to wipe thc blood away, but Warren slapped it down.

'Where's McCoy?' snapped Warren viciously.

'I don't know,' moaned the doctor.

Hatred flared in Jake's face, he clenched his teeth, and parted his lips angrily as he slapped the doctor's face viciously with the back of his hand.

A long groan broke from the doctor's lips and blood ran from the corner of his mouth. 'How can I tell you when I don't know,' he whispered. 'I just don't know.'

Warren swung on his heel and walked across the room. His knuckles showed white as he clenched his hands controlling the temper of frustration which welled inside him.

Duncan and Mason stepped towards the battered doctor.

'Hold it,' snapped Warren. 'We're not goin' to get anythin' out of him. C'm on let's go. We'll be back, doc, don't think we've finished with you yet.' He turned and strode out of the room followed by his three sidekicks.

Warren's words were lost on the doctor. His brain pounded as if a thousand hammers were beating his head. The room was going round and round in front of his eyes, until the floor suddenly seemed to rise to meet him.

Abbe Clements had held herself fearfully in her room. Several times her hand rested on the knob of the door ready to throw it open to stop the brutal beating downstairs, but she remembered Doc Wilson's words and knew that if she revealed herself to Warren, it would only bring more anxiety and danger to Frank.

When she heard the front door slam, she ran down the stairs and was soon on her knees beside the doctor who was already gaining consciousness. Abbe hurried for some water and gently bathed the doctor's face. A long moan escaped from his battered lips, and his eyes flickered open painfully.

The girl made him lie still for a few minutes whilst she continued to tend to his wounds and then helped him into a chair.

Tears welled in her eyes as she gazed at the battered man. 'Oh, doc,' she whispered, 'how could they? You took this all for me; I feel awful.' She was on her knees beside his chair. He smiled painfully as he laid a hand on her shoulder.

'You are not to blame, my dear,' he said. 'It's my own fault that I'm in this plight.' He paused as he felt his lips tenderly.

'Don't talk any more now. Let me help you up to bed,' said Abbe.

Wilson struggled to his feet and as they crossed the room he paused. A worried look came to his face as he looked hard at Abbe.

'Warren didn't get to know you were here?' he asked anxiously.

Abbe shook her head. 'No, I did as you told me,' she replied.

'Good,' approved Wilson. 'We could leave now but if we do Warren will really be suspicious of me. I'm afraid he will be back, Abbe.'

Chapter Ten

Frank eased himself from the rock floor of the cave.

'Guess I'd better get back out there,' he said nodding towards the entrance to their hide-out.

He took Mark's plate along with his own and scraped the remains of their mid-day meal into the fire.

'How are you feeling?' he asked the wounded deputy.

'Much better, thanks,' answered Mark. 'I reckon we could move to-day.'

Frank grinned at his friend. 'Not likely,' he said. 'The wound's mendin' nicely and another day or so will do the trick.'

Mark tightened his lips in annoyance.

'But I'm holdin' you up an' Warren will be havin' all his own way in Santa Rosa,' he protested.

'We'll take care of Warren when the time comes,' reassured Frank, picking up his rifle.

'I could travel...' started Mark.

'Sure you could,' interrupted Frank, 'but

supposin' we run into Warren's men out there?' He looked hard at the young deputy. 'No we stay!'

Mark knew better than to argue further with the sheriff who walked to the entrance of the cave.

McCoy settled himself behind a heap of rocks from which he held an advantageous position overlooking the gully, and at the same time was sheltered from prying eyes above by the shelf of overhanging rock.

Overhearing Warren's orders to leave three men in the Flats had made Frank extra cautious, but it had meant a lonely vigil for him. His mind was often troubled by the thoughts of Abbe's safety, the problem of clearing his name, and ridding Santa Rosa of Warren's grip.

He searched the gully slowly for any sign of movement. All was still and Frank was tempted to sleep in the heat of the afternoon, but he knew he dare not relax fully during daylight.

The afternoon wore on and the sun seemed to be hotter than ever. Suddenly, he started as his rifle slipped from his grip. He shook his head sharply, annoyed that he had dozed even though only for a few moments. He wiped the sweat from his forehead and licked his parched lips. Narrowing his eyes against the glare he methodically examined the gully.

He stiffened sharply with surprise when he saw two horses close to a clump of rocks. Their riders stood in front of them holding the reins and appeared to be in deep conversation. They looked around and then slowly made their way along the gully. Frank, his rifle at the ready, watched them carefully, wondering if these were the men Warren had left to patrol the Flats, and, if so, where was the third man?

A quarter of an hour passed before the two men who had moved along the gully searching the ground came to a halt. They dropped to their knees and examined the ground more carefully. Frank tensed himself; he realised they must have seen some tracks and this suspicion was confirmed when he saw one of them point in the direction he and Doc Wilson had taken to the path up the hillside. The two men straightened and gazed at the hill. Frank drew a sharp breath when he saw the taller rider point towards the cave. He scrambled away from the rocks and hurried to his deputy.

'Mark, two hombres have a spotted the cave,' he informed the wounded man.

The deputy looked startled, but answered coolly. 'We can hold 'em off.'

Frank smiled. 'Sure,' he said, 'but first you're goin' to stay here an' take no part in this; secondly, there should be three an' there's no tellin' where the other one is so we'll hev to move an' you'll need all your strength.'

The sheriff halted the protestations which sprang to Mark's lips by passing him his gun belt. Mark smiled as he drew the Colt from its holster.

'Thet's just in case you need it,' said Frank curtly. 'You stay here.' He turned quickly and hurried back to the cover of the rocks at the entrance to the cave. He saw that the two men had reached the path and were coming slowly up the hillside. Frank tensed himself watching every movement. As they drew nearer, he recognised them as two of Warren's sidekicks and he looked around for any sign of the third man.

A movement a little way inside the cave made Frank turn sharply. Mark's horse had grown restless and Frank watched it anxiously hoping it would settle down. The wounded deputy had noticed it too, and started to struggle to his feet to go to comfort it when a long shrill whinny broke the silence.

Frank swung his attention back to the two men and saw them freeze in their tracks. They looked sharply upwards towards the cave and then moved swiftly to the cover of some boulders. The sheriff watched the rocks carefully and five minutes passed before he noticed a movement about fifty yards to the right of the position in which he had last seen the men. He waited a moment and saw one of his pursuers crawling Indian fashion below the path. Franks raised his rifle and gently squeezed the trigger. Dust spurted in front of the man's nose and the startled cowboy flattened himself to the ground. In answer to Frank, four shots flew in his direction from the cover of the boulders. Frank shrank behind his cover as the bullets ricocheted off the rocks and when he eased himself up again the man below the path was nowhere to be seen. The sheriff peered cautiously over the rocks. Nothing appeared to move on the hillside but Frank knew that with plenty of cover two men, who would stop at nothing to kill him, were closing in on the cave.

Frank realised he must change his position but there was little cover immediately sur-rounding the rocks at the entrance to their hide-out. He detected a movement down the hillside and sent two quick shots in its direction. Immediately he had squeezed the trigger the second time he jumped to his feet and bending double hurled himself across the ten yards to a group of boulders. Bullets spanged the hillside around him and he flung himself forward driving the breath from his body as he hit the hard ground behind the boulders. He lay panting for a few moments and when he breathed more easily he recovered his sombrero and reviewed his new position. From this point he had more cover available and he reckoned he would be able to work his way down the hillside and deal with the man below him. He looked round anxiously, searching in vain for the second man whose last known position had been behind the group of boulders.

Frank moved slowly but steadily in Indian fashion down the hillside. He worked his way forward from cover to cover pausing every now and then to search the foreground. McCoy had moved at an angle to the last known position of the man he was stalking and when he paused behind a small mound of rocks, he detected a movement slightly below him and a little way to his left. He eased himself slowly round and brought his rifle to his shoulder. He waited patiently, hardly daring to breathe. The man slowly eased his way from between two rocks. Frank took careful aim, and gently squeezed the trigger, but at the same moment the man increased his pace and the bullet whined over his legs. The cowboy spun round, astonishment and fear flooding his face, at this unexpected attack. Frank's second bullet thudded into the man's chest before he had time to level his gun at the sheriff. He slumped back against the rock, his gun slipped from his grasp, and he slid slowly to the ground to lay still.

Frank's shots drew the unwelcome attention of the second man and bullets crashed around McCoy as he dived back to cover. Judging the direction of the firing Frank estimated that the cowboy had moved above the path intending to come down near the cave. He realised that he must work his way back up the hillside but once he started to move his pursuer's rifle broke the silence and lead flew around him. The man was in an advantageous position and Frank knew unless he acted quickly the cowboy would move further above him so that the cover to the cave would be of little use.

The sheriff poked his rifle round the edge of the rock, loosed off three quick shots, and crawled quickly forward to the cover of some bushes before bullets flew in his direction. Dust spurted near his knees, too close to be comfortable, and Frank realised he was dealing with a man who knew how to use a rifle. A bullet crashed through the bush close to Frank's head. He dived away from the bush for the cover of some rocks to his right, but the marksman was as quick as Frank and he felt his rifle torn from his grasp as a bullet thudded into it smashing the barrel. Frank rolled over in the dust and wiped the sweat from his forehead as he lay behind the rocks. He pulled his Colt from its holster realising he was now at a dis-advantage and would have to get nearer the man on the hillside.

A shot crashed across the gully and a brief moment passed before Frank realised the bullet had not come in his direction. He peered cautiously round the rocks. Gasping in amazement he leaped to his feet and started running towards the cave.

Mark leaned against the rock face at the mouth of the cave a smoking Colt in his hand watching the body of Warren's sidekick rolling down the hillside amidst a shower of dust and stones.

Frank scrambled quickly up the broken ground to Mark's side. 'You all right?' he panted as he reached the deputy.

Mark nodded. 'When I saw you move away from the cave I figured I'd better come and have a look.'

'As well you did,' said Frank thankfully. 'Thet hombre had got above me an' he was hot with a rifle.'

'Reckon he got a surprise when I pumped lead at him,' grinned Mark as they turned back into the cave.

Frank looked serious. 'We're goin' to have to move now,' he said. 'Think you can make it?'

'Sure,' Mark answered brightly, although his legs felt weak and his wound throbbed madly.

'It would have been better if we could have stayed another day at least but there's another of Warren's sidekicks somewhere out there an' when he finds the bodies...' Frank left the sentence unfinished as another thought crossed his mind. 'You know Mark, I've been trying to figure out why he wasn't with those two.' He paused thoughtfully. 'Maybe they discovered thet hombre Doc Wilson killed and he's high-tailed it to Warren.'

'If thet's the case,' said Mark, 'then we'd better get out of here quick; Warren'll bring a pack of cowpokes into the Flats.'

Frank saddled the horses quickly whilst Mark packed some of their belongings. They were soon ready for the trail and Frank helped Mark into the saddle before mounting his own horse. They followed the path by which they had reached the cave and once in the gully they urged their animals upwards to reach the trail out of the Flats. The two men put their horses into a steady trot once they were on the better ground but Frank kept an anxious eye on the trail ahead expecting the appearance of Warren.

His vigilance did not go unrewarded and he drew rein when he saw a cloud of dust moving rapidly towards the Flats.

'We've got to hide, Mark,' he said pointing in the direction of the riders who were still out of sight beyond the Flats.

The sheriff and his deputy left the trail and rode to a clump of stunted trees and rocks about a hundred yards from the trail where they slipped from the saddles and tied their horses to a tree. They watched the riders approaching at a fast gallop and as they drew near Mark moved back to the horses and held his hands over their nostrils whilst soothing them with soft words. Frank watched the riders thunder past on the trail and once they had disappeared into the Flats he hurried to Mark.

'Warren, Holliday, Duncan and Mason,' he said. 'We'll get out of here fast.'

They untied the horses and once they were in the saddles they put them into a fast pace away from Pintada Flats. Frank kept the animals at a full gallop but he watched Mark carefully for any sign of distress or weakness which the hard ride might cause the wounded man. The deputy was aware of Frank's attention and he gritted his teeth determined to last out the ride for he knew any faltering on his part would lessen their chances of escape and the last thing he wanted was for Frank to be recaptured by Warren. He knew if this happened Warren would return to Santa Rosa with a dead prisoner using the excuse that the killing had been in the execution of pursuit of a criminal.

Mark never knew how he survived the ride. After a few miles his arm went numb and his body began to feel as if it was being beaten by a thousand hammers. He felt as if he just wanted to lie down and leave everything to take care of itself but somehow he remained upright in the saddle across the desert and across the grasslands both of which seemed unending to the wounded man.

Frank's eyes were continually probing the blue distance as they rode on but he saw no sign of movement. He took a route which kept Santa Rosa just below the horizon and gradually they circled the town until they neared the trail from Fort Sumner to Santa Rosa. They slowed their sweating horses to a walk and eased their aching bodies in the saddles, thankful that the burning sun was losing some of its power as it was sinking in the west. Their shadows were long as they approached the road using what little cover offered itself.

Frank reconnoitered the trail whilst Mark enjoyed the relief of a halt amongst some trees. Finding the way clear Frank waved Mark forward and once across the road the two men put their horses into a steady, easy pace for about a quarter of a mile before swinging left and riding parallel with the road towards Santa Rosa. After a mile had passed Frank indicated a light shining in the darkness which now covered the country-side of New Mexico.

'That's Silas Linden's,' said Frank, relief

showing in his voice at the sight of their destination.

They slowed their horses to a walk and swung towards the light. Suddenly, Mark put an arresting hand on Frank's arm and halted their mounts.

'I'm not so sure we can trust old Silas,' he whispered.

'Why?' asked Frank, astonished that this suggestion should come at this stage of their plans.

'It puzzled me how Warren got on to our trail so quickly when I took Abbe to Fort Sumner,' explained Mark. 'I'll bet the answer's there,' he went on, nodding towards Silas's house. 'I never gave the old man a thought when we rode this way; reckon he saw us and when Warren came to the fork in the trail, a dollar or two would persuade Silas to remember what he had seen.'

Frank nodded. 'You could be right,' he agreed, 'but we've no proof, besides, we've got to trust him; we've got to have somewhere to go, and you're about all in. What Warren can do with a dollar so can we.' Frank was about to send his horse forward when Mark halted him again.

'Don't forget Gloria Linden is Warren's girl friend,' he pointed out.

Frank smiled. 'I know,' he said, 'but it's generally known that Silas frowns upon the association. Drink brought him to where he is. The old man still has some pride and remembers the ranch he used to have, and what he would have liked Gloria to be.' He paused a moment thoughtfully. 'C'm on,' he added wearily, 'we've got to risk it.'

Mark suddenly feeling the weariness of their long ride overwhelm him, slumped in the saddle and would have slipped from the horse had not Frank leaned forward quickly and supported him.

Mark shuddered, and straightened himself. 'Sorry,' he muttered. 'Guess you're right,' he grinned wearily at Frank. 'We've about had enough.'

They eased their horses slowly forward and halted them against the broken-down fence. Frank slipped from the saddle.

'Stay mounted,' he whispered to Mark, 'whilst I have a look round.'

He drew his Colt and slid through the hole in the fence and silently approached the dilapidated house. He trod carefully as he mounted the broken verandah, and crept forward towards the uncurtained window which allowed a pool of light to spill across the boards. Edging his way close to the wall, he peered into the room and was relieved to find that the sole occupant was Silas Linden, who was seated at the table toying with half a tumbler of whisky.

Frank turned and made his way swiftly but silently back to Mark.

'It's all right,' he said, helping the wounded man from the saddle. 'There's only Silas there.'

They tied their horses to the fence and crossed the overgrown garden to the door at the front of the house. Frank tried the door and finding it open the two men stepped into the hall. A chink of light showed under a door, and as it was thrown open a startled, red-eyed, Silas looked up to see two dust-covered, travel-stained, weary cowboys in front of him.

He stared at them in amazement. Slowly, his eyes focussed on them. 'Sheriff McCoy!' he gasped. 'I thought…'

'Never mind what you thought,' interrupted Frank. 'We need your help and need shelter.'

The urgency of the sheriff's tone penetrated the drink-numbed brain of the broken-down rancher. His mind and eyes cleared and Frank saw him start when he saw Mark's wound which had been aggravated by the ride.

'But if Warren finds you here...' Silas started to protest but again Frank interrupted him.

'He'll not find us here,' snapped Frank. 'That is unless you tell him,' he added.

The implication behind the words was not lost on the old man and anger smouldered in his eyes. It was banished as Frank continued.

'There'll be no mean reward if you help us,' said the sheriff who smiled to himself as he saw Silas's eyes brighten.

'What do you want me to do?' he asked.

'First, we want to hide out here,' replied Frank. 'The rest will follow in the morning after we've had a good night's rest.'

The conversation was halted as Mark fell forward against the table and slid to the floor with a dull thud.

'Quick, give me a hand,' snapped Frank bending over the still form of his deputy. 'He's fainted.'

Silas scraped his chair backwards and staggered round the table. He grabbed Mark's legs and Frank grasped the deputy under his arms. They carried him to the room indicated by Silas.

'Allus keep it ready in case Gloria comes

back,' he muttered.

They laid Mark on the bed and Silas soon had some hot water and Frank made his friend comfortable for the night. When he returned to the room Silas was busy preparing a meal and in this fact Frank saw a faint hope that they had an ally. Without a word he left the house and stabled the horses. He returned to find a meal ready for him and Silas seated at the table the whisky glass in his hand.

Frank crossed the room slowly, and picked up the glass and the bottle.

Silas stared incredulously at him. 'Thet's mine,' he slurred. 'Gimme me whisky.' He reached at the bottle, but Frank pulled it out of his reach.

'Silas,' he said grimly. 'There are serious things to talk about in the morning an' I want you sober!'

The old man said nothing, knowing it would be useless against the determination showing in the sheriff's face, but as he watched Frank sit down hatred smouldered in his eyes.

Chapter Eleven

As Jake Warren put his broad-chested horse into a fast run from Santa Rosa he cursed the stubbornness of Doc Wilson. Although the doctor denied all knowledge of the death of Roy Manners and the whereabouts of McCoy, Stevens, and the girl, Warren felt that Wilson knew the answers to his questions.

Mason, Duncan, and Holliday, ranged themselves alongside Warren and the earth shook with pounding hoofs as they raced past Pintada Mesa and into Pintada Flats. They kept their horses at a fast pace unaware that their entry into the Flats was being watched. As they moved deeper into the rough country their pace slackened and they kept a sharp look out for signs of the three riders who were patrolling the Flats.

Suddenly, two shots echoed in the gully to their right and as one man they hauled their horses to a halt. Warren moved nearer to the edge of the hill, his eyes searching the gully which stretched away below them.

'Over there,' he yelled pointing in the direction of a lone rider.

'Thet's Sam Baker,' shouted Red. 'I'd know his sit of horse anywhere.'

Warren frowned as he watched the man in the gully. 'There are two riderless horses down there,' he called. 'C'm on let's find out what's happened.' He pulled his horse round and soon the four men were following a path down the hillside into the gully.

Once they reached the bottom they pushed their horses forward quickly and were soon pulling their mounts to a standstill beside Baker. Warren gasped when he saw the body of his cowhand.

'What happened?' he asked sharply.

'Don't know,' answered Sam. 'I hed my meal after you'd left the ranch an' then high tailed back here. Zeke said they'd search this gully so I knew where to find 'em. Didn't reckon on this.' He paused and seeing Warren looking round he nodded his head towards a clump of rocks. 'Zeke's over there; shot through the chest,' he said. 'I saw you on the hill an' loosed off a couple of shots to attract your attention.'

'Reckon they'd found McCoy,' scowled Warren, 'an' paid fer their discovery.'

'Could hev been in thet cave,' observed

Duncan indicating the cave up the hillside.

'Yeah,' muttered Warren. 'Check it, Red.'

The foreman hurried up the hill and soon returned to report that the cave had been used but was now empty.

'McCoy an' the others hev made a run fer it after the killin',' said Warren a half smile flicking his face. 'I reckon they'll flee the country, they won't dare come near Santa Rosa now.'

'What about the Clements girl?' asked Mason.

'If she's gone with McCoy she'll be out of our way,' answered Jake. 'If she returns to Santa Rosa we can arrange a little reception for her.' He grinned as he pulled his horse round. 'C'm on I think a drink is called fer.'

The bunch of horsemen rode to Santa Rosa at a steady pace and it was late afternoon when they pulled up outside the Ace of Spades. As the evening wore on the tables began to fill up and the bar soon had plenty of occupants. Satisfied that all was going well Jake Warren left the Ace of Spades and rode towards his ranch and Gloria Linden at a gentle trot. Darkness was filling the countryside and lights shone from his house, but the feeling of elation would not have been so great had he known that at that same moment two weary men were moving cautiously towards a light at Silas Linden's.

It was mid-morning before Frank woke. The vigil in Pintada Flats and the wearing ride on top of the worry had taken their toll. It took a few moments before he realised where he was, but when he turned and saw the still sleeping form of Mark, he was soon on his feet and dressed. He hurried into the room to find Silas making some coffee.

'Thought you was goin' to sleep all day,' muttered Silas. 'Coffee will soon be ready; put it on when I heard you git up.'

'Thanks,' replied Frank. He crossed to the window and peered cautiously outside before hurrying to the door and swilling himself in the trough outside.

When he returned he enjoyed the coffee which Silas poured for him. He did not say a word, but watched the old man closely as he pottered about. After finishing his drink Frank shaved and then prepared a meal. Hardly a word had passed between the two men in all this time.

'Have some with me,' said Frank as he put two plates on the table.

The old man murmured his thanks and sat down. Frank noted Silas's eyes light up at the offer and thought that it was now time to put forward his suggestions.

'Silas, how would you like to get back on your feet again, to run this ranch as you used to do?' asked Frank quietly.

The old man's face brightened. He looked hard at Frank.

'You ain't jokin' boy?' he said suspiciously.

'No,' replied Frank. 'It would need some effort on your part and...'

'A fair amount of money,' interrupted Silas.

'Suppose that could be arranged?' said Frank.

A faraway look came into the old man's eyes. He could see this house, large and elegant the way it had been before his wife died, the rich grassland grazed by huge herds of cattle. Suddenly his gaze swung on Frank.

'It's impossible,' he muttered dejectedly.

'It isn't,' replied Frank. 'I could fix it. You still own the land, don't you?'

'Shore,' answered Silas, 'that's somethin' I never sold. Warren pestered me to sell until he gave up. Guess it didn't matter to him anymore when his longhorns graze it free anyway; they jest moved on to it when I hed no more cattle an' I couldn't stop him.'

'We'll hev cattle – your cattle on it again,' said Frank enthusiastically.

'There's some catch in this,' observed Silas eyeing the young sheriff suspiciously.

'Jest want you to hide us and get information,' said Frank. 'We can't go into Santa Rosa. I'm prepared to pay high in order to clear myself of the killin' of Mal Clements.' He paused to let his words sink in. 'There's just one thing,' he added. 'You'll hev to lay off the booze.'

Silas looked up sharply. 'But…' he started to protest.

'It can make you talk too much,' pointed out Frank strongly, 'and thet…'

'But if you want information,' interrupted Silas. 'I'll hev to go in the Ace of Spades. Folks'll be suspicious if I don't drink.'

'All right,' conceded the sheriff. 'But if you do, control it. Surely that's worth doin' to become a respected rancher again.'

The old man's eyes gleamed again. He straightened himself in his chair. 'All right,' he called slapping the table with his hand. 'I'll do it!'

'Good,' said Frank. 'First thing I want you to do is to go to Doc Wilson's and tell him we're here.'

'Isn't thet risky?' asked Silas. 'Warren gits

a lot of information from the doc.'

Frank stared at Silas in amazement. 'How do you know?' he said.

Silas grinned. 'I jest gits to know,' he whispered pleased with his secret.

Frank shrugged his shoulders. 'You'll find the doc's all right now.' He paused. 'He'd better be,' he added, 'he's got Miss Abbe with him.'

Silas laughed. 'Thet's one over Warren, Miss Clements being right under his nose and him not knowing.'

'We hope he doesn't,' replied Frank. 'You get off with my message an' see thet they are all right.'

The old man nodded and picking up a dirty battered sombrero shuffled to the door. Frank watched him go to the stable, come out with his only horse and turn on the trail towards Santa Rosa. As he watched him go the sheriff wondered if he had been right to trust old Silas.

It was late afternoon before Silas returned to find Frank and Mark, who was feeling much better after his long rest, anxiously awaiting his return.

'Wondered where you'd got to,' said Frank irritated at the long delay in news from town. 'Shouldn't hev taken you this long to get to Doc Wilson's and back.'

Silas did not speak, but eyed Frank coolly as the sheriff got up from his chair and peered cautiously out of the window at the front of the house. As he turned away from the window Silas threw his sombrero on to a chair.

'You've got a suspicious mind McCoy,' he said icily. 'I ain't brought anyone back with me.'

'Why hev you taken so long?' asked Frank testily as he sat down against the table.

Silas leaned across the table and looked hard at Frank. 'You sent me on a job, didn't you?' he hissed. 'Wal, I did it an' it wasn't as easy as it sounds.'

Frank and Mark glanced sharply at each other and looked at Silas questioningly.

'Warren's put a couple of cowpokes on to watch the Doc's an' it was some time before I could dispose of one at the back and get to the back door without being seen.'

The sheriff gasped. 'Warren watching the Doc's?'

'It was a fool thing to do to kill one of them,' scowled Mark.

'I'm not a greenhorn,' remarked Silas contemptuously. 'I didn't say I killed him. I only put him cold an' I took his roll of bills to make it look like a robbery.'

The two lawmen leaned forward on the table staring at Silas in amazement. A grin split Frank's face.

'Smart work, Silas,' he said.

The old man straightened himself proudly and nodded curtly at the two men in front of him.

'Couldn't get a reply for some time. Eventually my persistent knocking brought Miss Clements to the door; 'pears she was opening the door to no one but when she told the doc who it was he thought it might be all right.'

'How was she?' asked Frank anxiously.

'Abbe's all right,' replied Silas, 'but the doc's had a rough beatin' from Warren.'

'What!' gasped Mark and Frank together.

'Some time yesterday Warren arrived with those two hired guns an' Red Holliday. Thought Wilson knew something about you but he didn't talk an' Abbe kept out of sight.'

'Good,' said Frank somewhat relieved, 'but if Warren's goin' to play it rough with the doc then he'll hev it rougher from us.'

'Where hev you been since leavin' Doc Wilson's?' asked Mark.

'You gittin' suspicious again?' snorted Silas. 'Wal, to settle your mind, I've been at the Ace of Spades. Tryin' to git some information,' he added hastily as he noted Mark's suspicious look.

'Wal, what's new in town?' asked Mark.

'Warren appears to be taking things steady. He has the town where he wants it an' can move slowly especially as he's spreadin' it around thet you'll have fled the country after the other killings in the Flats.'

'Good work, Silas,' approved Frank eagerly. 'If Warren is movin' in slowly so as not to alarm the town then its to our advantage; it gives us more time.'

'I'll go into town again, to-morrow,' said Silas as he crossed to the door. 'Jest goin' to put my horse away.'

A few moments later Silas burst into the room.

'Quick,' he panted, 'out of sight. Some hombre comin' along the south road.'

Mark hurried to the bedroom whilst Frank crossed to the window and peered cautiously out. The outline of the distant lone rider indicated a man who looked weary with travel; he was slumped in the saddle but every now and then he would straighten and look around.

'Shore ain't in a hurry,' muttered Silas.

Frank didn't answer, but watched the man

carefully as he came nearer. Suddenly he let out a shout which startled Silas beside him and brought Mark hurrying from the bedroom.

'It's Dan!' yelled Frank, his eyes lighting up as his face opened with a broad smile.

'Whose Dan?' asked Silas.

'My brother,' replied Frank. 'Go and fetch him in,' he added bustling the old man to the door.

Silas stepped out on to the broken verandah and stood waiting the arrival of the rider. As he approached Silas saw that both man and animal were tired; both were covered in dust and the horse seemed thankful when its rider halted it in front of Silas.

'Evenin',' greeted the horseman. 'Is it much further to Santa Rosa?'

'Not very far,' replied Silas casually, 'but there's no need to go there to-night, Dan.' A smile parted Silas's lips when he saw the startled look on the man's face.

'How do you know my name?' asked Dan, suspicious and alert now in spite of his weariness.

'Slip off thet saddle an' step inside to meet your brother,' replied Silas with a grin.

Dan was out of the saddle in a flash, across the boards, and into the house.

'Frank!' he yelled, when he saw his brother standing near the table.

'Dan!' shouted Frank and leaped to grasp his brother's hand and clap him on the back. 'It's shore good to see you!'

'What's this mess you're in?' asked Dan seriously.

'Tell you about it shortly,' answered Frank. 'You'll want a clean-up and a feed, but first of all meet Mark Stevens, my deputy, and Silas Linden who's one of the only two townsfolk thet trusts me.'

As the two men shook hands with Dan they saw a slim, tall man of about twenty five and in spite of the dust they detected a clean cut face set with sharp, steel blue eyes which missed nothing. Silas noted the long supple fingers as he took his hand and guessed that if the necessity arose they would be quick to draw the Colt which hung low on his hip in a plain leather holster tied to his leg with a thin thong.

Frank made Dan's horse comfortable for the night whilst Silas prepared a meal and Dan cleaned himself up. It was not long before Dan was in full possession of all the events. He had made no comments whilst he heard the story, but as he pushed his empty plate away from him and sat back in the chair to roll a cigarette he looked round the three men.

'Seems this Warren's goin' to be a tough one to crack especially with those hired guns around. I've heard of those two but never tangled with them; pretty useful with a gun from what I've heard.' He paused to light the cigarette. 'Seems to me the best thing will be to get on the inside.'

The three men stared at him incredulously.

'Inside?' asked Mark.

Dan blew a cloud of smoke into the air and nodded. 'Yeah. Me!'

'I'll not let you take that risk,' protested Frank.

'I'm here to help you clear up this mess, an' I think thet's the way to do it, I can't see us doin' it from the outside.'

Silas watched Dan, admiring the cool way he had accepted the facts and made his decision. 'You know,' he said. 'I think Dan's right.'

Before Frank could protest further Dan pushed himself from his chair. 'I'm pretty weary,' he said, 'I'm turning in; we'll sleep on it to-night but I reckon it'll hev to be an inside job.'

The light was fading from the sky the next day when Dan McCoy first rode into Santa Rosa. The town was beginning to adapt itself to its night-life; lights were coming on in various windows; the stores were closed for the night and already several horses were tied to the rail outside the Ace of Spades. Dan swung from his horse as he brought it to a halt before the imposing front of the saloon. He strolled casually on to the sidewalk and pushed his way through the door. The huge room was beginning to fill up. Many of the tables were already occupied and the gambling section had attracted many cowboys eager to try to increase their pay roll.

Dan walked slowly between the tables pausing every now and then to watch the progress of some game, but his eyes kept searching the room for the men described by Frank. He was watching a faro game when the door opened to admit five cowboys led by a tall broad shouldered man who tipped his hat off his forehead as he strode between the tables towards the bar. Dan stiffened when he saw the red hair and quickly ran his eye over the man whose features fitted those of Red Holliday. As they reached the bar the barmen were quick to do their bidding.

McCoy continued to move slowly towards the bar and grunted satisfactorily to himself when he saw a door open and three men stroll into the room. The first one was dark, his hair sleek and a thin dark moustache covered his top lip. He was hatless and contentedly smoked a long cigar as he looked satisfactorily round the room. The two men who were with him were shabbily dressed by comparison with their companion whose red silk shirt and black trousers were immaculate. Dan saw the tin stars pinned to dark brown shirts and knew that Warren and his hired guns had appeared on the scene. This was even better than he had hoped for.

He strolled up to the bar alongside Red Holliday who gave him only a cursory glance as he laughed at some joke made by one of his companions. Dan ordered a drink and as he turned away from the counter he knocked against Holliday spilling the beer down the cowboy.

Red spun round on Dan. His eyes were black with anger and without waiting for an apology he struck hard at Dan's face sending him sprawling across the floor.

'Careful what you do next time,' laughed Red who turned back to the bar amidst the raucous laughter of his cowboys. He picked up his glass of beer and took no notice of Dan who climbed slowly to his feet wiping the blood from his mouth with the back of his hand. Suddenly, he stepped forward and brought his palm up sharply against the bottom of Red's glass, sending it hard into the man's mouth and spilling the beer down his shirt.

Red spluttered as the beer choked his throat and he dropped his glass on the floor with a splintering crash. Before he could recover Dan crashed his fist into Red's face sending him staggering backwards against his companions who stopped him from hitting the floor. Three of the men went for their guns but they had hardly touched the butts when they saw themselves staring into the cold muzzle of Dan's Colt.

'Jest keep your hands off,' Dan warned casually. He saw Warren's hired guns move forward to exert the authority of the stars on their chests, only to be halted by Warren by an almost imperceptible shake of the head. 'Want any more?' drawled Dan as Red was pushed to his feet.

The foreman glared at him. 'You hev the upper hand,' he snarled indicating the gun.

'Tell your sidekicks to keep out of this an' we'll settle it ourselves,' replied Dan curtly.

Red looked hard at him for a moment. He saw a tall, slim man, neatly turned out whose clean cut features bore a trickle of blood where he had hit him. Red realised this man knew how to handle himself but he figured he had the advantage in size and weight.

A grin slowly split Red's lips and he reached down to unbuckle his gun belt. He handed it to the man beside him.

'Hold this,' he ordered. 'I'll want it in a minute when I've dealt with this coyote. And keep out of this,' he added, 'it's my quarrel.'

'Thanks,' said Dan and slipped his Colt back into its holster.

The saloon had gone deadly quiet. Cowboys had dragged some of the tables further back and the crowd formed a large arc with the bar on one side.

Dan unbuckled his belt and whilst he was occupied with taking it from his hips to put on the bar Red leaped forward, hurled his fist at Dan sending him crashing to the floor where he slid along the boards until he was stopped by the legs of the crowd. A gasp went from the crowd. Red's quick unfair move had taken them all by surprise. Dan lay still his head on one side. A loud laugh broke from Red's throat as he turned to the bar and yelled for a beer.

Dan stirred, shook his head, and before any of Holliday's sidekicks could shout a warning he hurled himself at the foreman. His arms encircled the big man's waist as his shoulder dug hard into his side. The two men crashed to the floor but just before they hit the wood Dan released his hold and rolled to one side. In a flash he leaped to his feet and as Red pushed his big frame from the board Dan jumped forward swinging his fist in a sharp upper cut to Red's chin twisting him round to the floor again. Dan stood over the foreman gasping for breath. His shoulders hunched, his arms hanging limp, he was unprepared for the sudden move of Holliday who twisted sharply and kicked Dan's feet from under him. Dan hit the floor hard driving the breath from his body. Before he could roll away Holliday hurled himself on top of Dan. His huge fist crashed into Dan's left eye. Pain shot through his head and he could feel the eye closing rapidly. With a yell of triumph Red drew his arm back and it was only just in time that Dan saw the fist hurling at his right eye. He twisted his head sideways feeling the fist shave his neck to pound onto the hard floor. Red yelled with pain as he felt some bones crack. Momentarily stunned by the painful shock his grip relaxed and Dan seized the opportunity to throw the heavy body off him. He twisted over on top of Red and rained heavy blows at the cowboy's face. Red struggled but Dan kept his grip and as Red raised his head Dan clipped him hard under the chin to jerk his head back. It hit the floor hard and Red moaned with pain. As Dan's fist hit him again he lost consciousness. Gasping for breath Dan pushed himself off the unconscious man. He grasped the edge of the bar and pulled himself up to slump against the counter. He called for two glasses of beer and shakingly raised one to his lips.

No one moved as they watched him. He told the barman to bring a bowl of water in which he bathed his hands and face. Suddenly, he picked it up and threw the contents into the face of the unconscious Red. Holliday stirred and spluttered. His eyes opened slowly and when he had raised himself on his elbows he shook his head trying to clear his brain. Two of the sidekicks stepped forward and helped him to his feet. Dan watched him, casually sipping his beer. Slowly Red's eyes focused on McCoy.

'Beer?' invited Dan indicating the full glass on the counter.

Suddenly, everyone started to talk at once and returned to their drinks and their gambling. The incident was finished.

Red staggered against the bar. 'Thanks,' he muttered between cracked lips as he picked up the glass. 'You shore pack a wallop.'

As Dan turned back to the bar he noted with satisfaction that Warren and his hired guns were moving in their direction.

'Thet was some fight,' said Jake Warren smoothly as he reached the two men who both turned to see who spoke. 'Red, you'll hev to take a few lessons from this hombre,' he added with a grin. He turned to Dan. 'I'm Jake Warren,' he said holding out his hand. 'Always pleased to know anyone who can fight an' pull a gun like you.'

Dan took his hand. 'Dan Ferguson,' he said. 'Guess you must own this place. I'm sorry fer any damage caused, if thet'll put me right with the law,' he added nodding at the two men with Warren.

'No charges if Mister Warren doesn't make them,' answered the taller of the two men.

'Fergit it,' said Warren. He glanced at Red. 'Bring him to my office when you've finished your beer,' he ordered.

Red nodded and Dan watched the three men cross the saloon to the door by which they had entered the room.

'Is this Warren a big shot?' asked Dan toying with his glass.

Red laughed. 'The biggest,' he replied.

'Where do you fit in?' asked Dan.'

'Nothin' to do with this joint,' answered Red. 'I'm foreman for him. He owns a big spread to the north an' west of town an' controls thet to the south. Only bit he doesn't own is the Lazy A to the east, but he soon will.' He drained his glass. 'C'm on we'd better not keep him waiting.'

Red led the way to Warren's office and Dan was impressed by the large well furnished room. Warren was seated behind a desk with the two gunmen on either side. He indicted two chairs for the newcomers and he looked hard at Dan before he spoke.

'Where you headin'?' he asked curtly.

'Nowhere particular,' replied Dan shrugging his shoulders. 'I was jest driftin' through.'

'Want to work fer me?' asked Warren.

'Depends,' said Dan casually.

'I've somethin' big comin' up an' I want men who can ride hard, fight hard an' use a gun,' he said. 'I pay well.'

Dan appeared to consider the matter. 'Guess I may as well if the money's good,' he answered casually.

'Good,' grinned Warren and introduced the three men to Dan. 'Right,' he went on. 'Your first job fer me is tell me where you got thet wallet, the one you used when you paid fer the drinks in the bar.'

Dan stared at Warren. 'What you want to know thet fer?'

Warren's eyes darkened. 'Men don't ask questions when they work fer me,' he snapped. 'They jest supply the answers.'

Dan did not reply but looked uneasily at Duncan and Mason. Suddenly Warren began to laugh. 'Scared of the law?' he asked. 'Don't worry about them they're a couple of my men.' He saw Dan stare disbelievingly at him. 'Things hev been happenin' around here an' we had to put Clay an' Ed in temporary. Now what about thet wallet?'

'Wal, you seem to hev things pretty well sewn up here so I guess there's no harm in tellin' you,' said Dan. 'I took it off a hombre along the trail.'

'Let me see it,' said the rancher.

Dan fumbled in his pocket and passed the wallet to Warren who turned it over examining it carefully. He passed it to Mason.

'F.M.' he said. 'Frank McCoy an' I've seen him use it in the Ace of Spades. Where did you meet up with him?'

'Between here an' Fort Sumner,' replied Dan.

'By himself?' asked Warren.

'No,' drawled Dan. 'Hombre with a badly shot arm an' a girl.'

'How did you git it?' said Warren.

'I edged up near their camp. Seemed to be planning a journey an' in the course of it they checked their cash. I was short so I strolled in with a gun thet jest made them want money no more.'

Warren stared incredulously at Dan. When he had recovered his surprise he asked Dan, 'The girl?'

'Wal, I figured I'd take her with me but she drew a gun on me and I'm afraid I fired first,' replied Dan casually.

Warren saw some disbelief in the eyes of the other three men.

'All right,' he said. 'We'll not pass judgment now.' He turned to Dan. 'If what you say is true, an' it seems likely from the possession of this wallet, then you've done me a good turn I'll not forget. Did you bury the bodies?'

Inwardly Dan stiffened. This was something he hadn't reckoned on. 'Shore,' he replied calmly. 'Didn't want to leave any evidence.'

'Where?' snapped Warren.

'On the hill above the crossing of Alamogordo Creek.'

'Check it to-morrow, Red!' ordered Warren.

Chapter Twelve

As he left the office with Red Holliday Dan puzzled as to how he could forestall Red's investigation of the hill above Alamogordo Creek. Warren had been careful to tie Dan's movements up by telling Red to give him a bunk at the ranch and a job until Duncan and Mason contacted him.

'There's no need to go right away,' grinned Red as they strolled into the saloon. 'Come an' hev a drink with the boys and meet some of the gorgeous girls thet adorn the Ace of Spades.'

Dan hoped that he might be able to slip away later but he realised Red Holliday drank very little and kept close to him.

'Not a drinkin' man either, Dan?' observed Red. 'Thet'll suit the boss, he likes his gunmen sober.'

'Any idea what job he's lining up fer me?' asked Dan.

'Vaguely, but I aren't sayin',' returned Red. 'You'll know soon enough, but I will say play along with Warren an' you'll be all right; he's a generous boss but he doesn't like mistakes. Fer instance there'd better be three graves on thet hill top.'

Dan did not reply, but turned his attention to the room whilst Red's interest centred on a girl who had just joined the party. As he raised his glass to his lips someone bumped into Dan's back. He spun round ready to call a cowboy out but his retort froze on his lips when he saw Silas. He felt like hugging the old man with joy, but outwardly he glared angrily.

'Watch it old man,' he snapped.

Silas muttered his apologies and touched his dirty sombrero.

'Silas,' yelled Red, 'meet our new rider Dan Ferguson. Buy him a drink, Dan, an' keep the right side of Silas, he's a gossipy old man.'

Dan called for a drink for Silas and awaited his opportunity to give Silas a message.

'You're in,' whispered Silas as the glass touched his lips.

Dan nodded. 'But in an awkward spot. Tell Frank to make three heaps of stones – graves on the hill above Alamogordo Creek early to-morrow.'

Silas frowned, puzzled by the message, but before he could query it Red Holliday slapped Dan on the back.

'C'm on Dan,' he said, 'time we got out to the Diamond D.'

Without a glance at Silas Dan brushed past him and followed Holliday from the saloon.

Although mystified by Dan's message Frank was up early the next morning and soon on the way to Alamogordo Creek, unaware that Red Holliday left the Diamond D ranch to take the same trail an hour later.

Frank's ride was uneventful. He proceeded speedily but cautiously and once above the Creek he hastily erected three mounds of stones as if they covered three graves. His task was almost complete when he was startled by the crash of a Colt. A bullet spanged the dirt in front of the stone he was about to pick up. Frank spun round, his hand reaching for his gun but it froze on the butt when he saw Red Holliday, a smoking Colt in his hand, step from the cover of some trees.

'I wouldn't if I were you, McCoy,' grinned Red. 'Thought you were meant to be under one of them,' he observed nodding to the heaps of stones.

Frank said nothing as he faced Red.

'Reckon I ought to pull this trigger an' put

you under but then I figure Mister Warren ought to see you,' said Red coolly. 'Ferguson's shore goin' to hev to answer some questions.'

The red headed foreman started to walk slowly towards Frank who, realising the desperate situation, tensed himself for any opportunity of escape which might present itself. Holliday was about fifteen yards from him when his foot stubbed against a half hidden stone. Momentarily his balance was disturbed and his gun wavered. Frank seized the slim opportunity. Like lightning he flung himself sideways, dragging at his Colt. Red's gun spat lead at the diving man and Frank felt a sharp stab in his left forearm as a bullet nicked his flesh, but already he was rolling over on the hard ground and as he turned on to his stomach he squeezed the trigger. He saw the look of surprise cross Holliday's face, his hand clasp his chest and his knees begin to buckle. He slumped forward onto his knees endeavouring to aim his Colt at Frank but his bullets slapped harmlessly into the ground in front of him. The gun slipped from his grasp and Red fell forward into the dust. Wearily Frank pushed himself to his feet and walked slowly towards the man on the ground, keeping his gun ready in case of any trick.

When he reached Holliday, he turned him over with his foot and seeing that he was dead he slipped his Colt back into his holster. He sighed deeply as he turned away and slapped the dust from his clothes before finishing his task of erecting the mock graves.

As he worked he puzzled over the appearance of Red Holliday. He could only guess that Warren had wanted some proof of Dan's story of the killings and had sent Holliday to check on the graves. Deciding that it would not do for Holliday's body to be found beside the graves, Frank found the foreman's horse and slung him over the saddle. He rode about four miles in the direction of Santa Rosa and dumped the body a hundred yards from the trail. His unpleasant task completed, he sent his horse at a fast gallop to Silas Linden's dilapidated house.

'We ought to warn Dan,' said Silas concerned by Frank's story.

'Dan'll know soon enough,' replied Frank, 'besides, we'll never get near him; if I know Warren he'll hev kept a close watch on Dan whilst Red checked his story.'

'Even though Red's dead, Warren will hear about the graves an' thinkin' Abbe's dead, he'll start to move in on the Clements property right away,' pointed out Mark.

'Yeah,' agreed Frank, 'an' I figure we ought to move in first.'

As Dan watched Red Holliday ride away, he wondered if Silas and Frank had understood the message. If not, the whole set up could blow sky high and at the moment there was nothing he could do about it. The day was an uneasy one for Dan, until late in the afternoon his attention was drawn to two horses ridden at a fast pace towards the ranch. His eyes narrowed when he saw Clay Duncan and Ed Mason ride straight to the ranch house to pull up in a swirl of dust. Both men dropped quickly out of the saddles, and climbed the steps on to the verandah to be admitted to the house a moment after their knock on the door had been answered. A few minutes passed before Clay Duncan strode from the house and hurried towards the corral where Dan was busy.

'Ferguson,' shouted Duncan. 'Boss wants to see you.'

Dan caught up with the gunman as he reached the steps. Duncan motioned him forward and Dan entered the house. After the gunman had closed the door behind him he nodded towards a door. When Dan entered the room he noted that Duncan stayed against the door and Mason was standing to the right which put him almost directly behind Dan when he faced Warren across a huge desk. One slip now and Dan knew he was in as tight a spot as he had ever been in.

For a moment the rancher did not speak but stared hard at Dan who held the man's gaze.

'When the stage from Fort Sumner arrived in town it brought Red Holliday's body.' Warren's voice was low, his tone even and cold. His eyes narrowed studying Dan's reaction.

'What!' Dan gasped, surprise and amazement filling his face. 'Who did it?'

'Thet's what we'd like to know,' hissed Warren savagely. 'He was found close to the trail about four miles this side of Alamogordo Creek. Know anything about it?'

'Me?' Dan's eyes widened with surprise.

'Only us four knew he was goin' thet way,' pointed out Warren.

'Thet don't mean any of us killed him,' rapped Dan, annoyance that Warren should suspect him showing on his face. 'I certainly couldn't. You know I've been around here all day, you made sure of thet by the job you gave me.'

Some measure of relief came to Dan when he saw Warren relax. 'Guess I did,' replied the rancher, his tone more normal. 'It jest seemed strange thet he should be gunned down when checkin' your story.' He turned to the two gunmen. 'All right boys, sit down. I guess Dan's in the clear.' Warren handed round cheroots and after they had been lit he spoke again. 'The stage also brought news about the graves so as Abbe Clements is dead I'm figurin' on speedin' things up. I was content to bide my time but there's no need now.' He paused a moment drawing at his cheroot. He leaned forward on the desk glancing at the two hired guns. 'You two completed the first part of my plans your first night here, now with Dan to help you you start in on the second part.' He drew at his cheroot and as he did so Dan sensing he was close to some information spoke up.

'Is there any link between the two parts?' he asked.

Warren looked sharply at him. 'I told you once before not to ask leading questions. What's happened is no concern of yours, it's what's goin' to happen thet is.'

'What's the plan boss?' asked Mason.

'You can run it as you like; all I want is

results an' thet means thet the Lazy A spread becomes mine.' Warren pushed himself from his chair and walked to a map on the wall. 'C'm here an' I'll show you the lay out.'

The three men gathered round the map.

'Santa Rosa's here,' said Warren pointing to the map. 'The Diamond D borders it on the north and west. On the south is Silas Linden's spread. The drunken old sot won't sell. He has no cattle and as I graze it free it's as good as mine.'

'Thet means if you get the Lazy A you encircle the town,' gasped Dan, 'an' you can run things as you like.'

Warren grinned. 'You catch on fast Ferguson.' He strolled back to his chair. 'Mind you,' he said, 'there are other reasons for having the Lazy A but they don't concern any of you. Jest make sure I get it.'

'Right, boss,' said Duncan. 'Jest tell us who owns it an' we'll use a little persuasive power.' He laughed loud as he struck his right fist hard against the palm of his left hand.

'Thet's jest the snag,' snapped Warren. 'No one knows who owns it, not even the foreman. He was hired by letter. You are just goin' to hev to persuade those cowpokes thet it isn't worth while stayin' on out there.

When the place is empty I'll move in an' thet'll bring the owner into the open if he hasn't come before.'

Warren's laugh of triumphant satisfaction rang in Dan's ears as he swung into the saddle and turned his horse alongside Duncan and Mason to ride east from the Diamond D. The rancher's outline of his plans tallied with Franks theories of Warren's bid for power but Dan was puzzled by the fact that Warren claimed there were other reasons for wanting the Lazy A

The three men kept their horses at a steady pace and after a few miles turned from the trail to cut across the grassland towards the Lazy A. A further five miles brought them to a slight rise in the land up which they rode steadily.

'Edge of Warren's land at top of this rise,' said Mason. 'We'll get a good look at the Lazy A spread from up there.'

When they reached the top of the rise they saw that the land dropped steeply but evenly before them levelling out about a mile below and rolling away in some of the best grassland Dan had ever seen. About twenty miles away the land rose again to level into scrub and desert broken by steep slopes and cliff-like mesas. Below them at the foot of the slope about half a mile to the right lay the ranch house, bunkhouse, stables and corrals of the Lazy A. Dan saw that the buildings and fences were in good repair and the ground around them clean and tidy; the whole place had an atmosphere of hard work. Several corrals were occupied by a large number of horses and out on the range Dan could see large herds of cattle.

'I figure our job's easier with the buildings at the foot of this slope,' observed Duncan.

'Yeah, it's a natural fer an attack,' agreed Mason. 'But I think we work easy, first stampede a few cattle, burn a stable or two, maybe the bunkhouse, and work over some of the cowpokes. If thet don't persuade them then we'll really let into the place.'

'What you doin?' asked Duncan turning to Dan who was writing on a piece of paper.

'Jest makin' a plan of the place – it will probably be useful to plan our operations,' replied Dan.

'Good idea,' praised Clay, 'but hurry it up it will soon be dark an' we want a closer look at the place.' He started to turn his horse along thc hill top.

'Hold it,' said Dan.

Both men turned in their saddles surprised by the sharpness in Dan's tone.

'You aren't figurin' on leavin' here without leaving our mark behind, are you?' asked Dan.

'We want the lie of the land first,' replied Mason.

'I've got all we want down here,' said Dan indicating his drawing.

'Let's hev a look,' snapped Mason turning his horse towards Dan and grabbing the sheet of paper from Dan's hand. 'Guess thet should do,' he agreed somewhat reluctantly.

'In thet case we may as well start on the job straight away,' Dan said searching the scene below. 'How about releasing those horses from the those three corrals?' he suggested.

Duncan laughed. 'Good idea,' he agreed. 'It'll put a problem to the Lazy A boys. We'll wait until the light fades an' then they'll hev some night work on their hands.'

The three men slipped from the saddles and moving below the sky line rolled themselves cigarettes. They stretched themselves on the ground and watched the sky darken. Fifteen minutes went by before Mason pushed himself to his feet.

'Reckon we can go now,' he said stretching himself. 'One corral each; let the horses out an' then away.'

Clay and Dan nodded their agreement and the three men swung into the saddles, slipped quickly over the skyline and rode slowly down the long slope. They watched the buildings carefully but there was no movement outside; the only evidence of life was the light and noise from the bunkhouse.

The riders split up as the slope flattened out and each made for the gate of a corral. Dan was the first to reach his position and he waited for the other two to reach theirs.

'Let 'em go!' Mason's voice split the darkness and the three men flung open the corral gates and with loud yells frightened the horses sending them shoving and pushing one against the other as they attempted to crowd through the gateway in their bid for a new found freedom.

Hoofs pounded the hard ground as the horses thundered towards the grassland and the open spaces. Each of the three men had tucked himself between the gate and fence for protection and now hung tightly to their own horses which struggled to tear themselves free to run with the other animals.

As the last horse tore out of the corral, Dan flung the gate shut, leaped into the saddle, and sent his horse into a fast gallop towards the hillside. The cry of the horses and the thunder of the hoofs had already brought cowboys running from the bunkhouse some of whom ran to the stables for their horses whilst others ran towards the corrals. Suddenly a gun flash split the darkness to be followed by four others. Dan glanced to his left and saw two silhouettes emerge from the blackness. As they approached him at a fast run he recognised Ed and Clay and when they drew alongside him he matched his pace to theirs.

When they reached the hillside the pace automatically slackened as the three men set their animals up the long slope. A yell broke out behind them and glancing back Dan saw four horsemen round the end of the buildings and send their mounts in fast pursuit.

The three men urged their horses faster and when they reached the top of the slope they put their mounts into an earth-shaking gallop towards Santa Rosa. The four Lazy A men quickened their mounts realising that they must close the gap or lose the men in the darkness. Dan saw them break the skyline as they came over the top of the hill but lost sight of them as they merged with the dark background of the earth behind them. The trail dipped into a hollow which ran along the hillside. As they reached the bottom of the hollow Dan turned off the trail and called to the others to follow him. After riding about a quarter of a mile along the hollow he pulled his horse to a halt.

'What's the idea?' snapped Clay as he drew alongside Dan.

'They won't see us in the dark,' he said, 'an' will stick to the trail – if they don't we've got these.' He patted his Colt and grinned at the two men.

They turned their horses and sat still listening to the hoofs which pounded nearer and nearer until they sounded to be almost on top of them. The three men drew their Colts reassuringly but slipped them back into the holsters when they heard the hoof-beats move across the hollow and climb out of it along the trail. When the pounding had faded in the distance the three men sent their horses out of the hollow and headed for Santa Rosa across country.

When they reached town they rode slowly along the main street and pulled to a halt outside the Ace of Spades. They swung from the saddles and beat the dust from their clothes before strolling casually into the saloon. They made their way to Warren's office where they found him talking to some of the men who ran the gaming tables. After he had dismissed them he listened with interest as Ed Mason told him their story.

'Thet's a good start,' he said. 'Hot it up an' the Lazy A will soon be mine.' He pushed himself out of his chair. 'I guess you could all do with a drink.'

He led the way from the office and the four men were enjoying their drinks when Dan noticed four dust covered riders come into the saloon. They crossed to the bar and Dan saw the tall fair-haired leader fix his eyes on Warren.

'Warren,' he snarled. His voice lashed along the bar. Silence settled over the cowboys nearby as they eased away from the counter. 'You've always threatened the Lazy A an' now it seems you've moved into action, but I'm goin' to settle this once and for all.'

The tall man went for his gun. He was fast on the draw but Dan was even faster and as the gun came out of the holster Dan's bullet crashed into it sending it spinning to the floor. The crowd gasped at the speed of Dan's draw and the Lazy A man stared incredulously as he held his wrist.

Warren moved slowly towards the cowboy, his eyes smouldering with anger. He drew his arm back and slapped the man viciously across the face.

'Don't come in here threatening me,' hissed Warren. 'Now get out an' tell thet boss of yours whoever he is that I am to take over the Lazy A if he won't sell out.'

The fair-haired man glared at Warren. 'We'll not move out,' he snapped. 'You'll hev to take it over our dead bodies.'

Warren laughed. 'An' thet's jest what we might do,' he said.

The four Lazy A men turned and walked to the door slamming it as they went out.

Warren turned to Dan. 'Thanks,' he said. 'Thet sure puts you right in with me.'

The four men turned back to their drinks and the Ace of Spades resumed its entertainment as if nothing had happened.

'Since Dan told us he'd killed Miss Clements I've been figuring that I can really get a grip on Clements' property,' said Warren as he toyed with a cheroot. He looked at Mason and Duncan. 'In a few minutes you two can pay a visit to the Clements' house an' bring back here all the documents you can find.'

The two men nodded and finished their drinks.

'What about Dan?' asked Mason.

'I'd like him to stick around here,' grinned

Warren. 'Jest in case the Lazy A come gunning again.'

Mason and Duncan left the saloon and Warren returned to his office, whilst Dan positioned himself so that he could see all around the room.

A few minutes passed before Dan saw the door open. Silas Linden came in and shuffled slowly to the bar near Dan. Silas got his drink before he spoke quietly without looking at Dan.

'Glad you're here,' he muttered. 'Thought you'd better know Frank an' Mark are trying to forestall Warren by removing all documents from Clements' house.'

'What!' Dan gasped in a whisper. 'When do they figure on trying it?'

'They're out there now!' replied Silas.

Chapter Thirteen

As darkness blanketed the countryside of New Mexico Frank McCoy and Mark Stevens slipped from the house, brought their horses, which Mark had saddled in daylight, and rode towards Santa Rosa. Silas Linden watched them go somewhat dubious that Frank should risk going to town. He agreed with the young sheriff that once Warren had accepted Dan's story of the killing of Abigail Clements he would move quickly to consolidate his hold on the Clements' property. Frank hoped to forestall Warren by removing any documents there may be in the Clements house. After an uneasy half hour Silas hurried to the stable, saddled his horse and rode at a fast trot towards town.

Frank and Mark kept their horses at a steady pace and as they neared town slipped away from the trail to circle and approach Clements' house from the back. They pulled their mounts to a halt under some trees about fifty yards from the house, but sat still for a few moments. When they were certain that all was quiet they slid from the saddles, stealthily approached the house and parted company to circle the house.

'No one about,' whispered Mark as they met on the front verandah.

'All clear this way,' reported Frank. 'We'll use a window,' he added. 'It's less likely to be noticed than if we force the door.'

They trod quietly along the boards and found a window the catch of which was easily forced. Opening the window they stepped over a low sill into a small room.

'Clements' study was across the hall,' whispered Frank. He felt his way carefully across the room, found the door and stepped into the darkened hall. Two strides took them across the hall to another door which admitted them to a large room. Frank and Mark drew the thick curtains across the two windows before Frank struck a match. By the spluttering glow he stepped to the desk where he applied the match to a lamp. He adjusted the wick until he dimmed the light to a brightness which was just sufficient for them to see by.

'You try the desk,' Frank said and turned his attention to a chest of drawers.

They worked swiftly but methodically through papers and documents, putting into their pockets those which they thought might be of some use to Warren. Mark tugged at a deep bottom drawer to find it locked. He pulled out his knife and had just prised open the drawer when he froze. A low squeak had come from the hall. He looked sharply at Frank who, having heard the noise, indicated to him to blow out the light. Mark glanced at the drawer and noticed a bundle of papers neatly tied with thin string. He grabbed them and blew out the light. Suddenly, the door was flung open and gun flashes split the darkness. Mark heard a bullet whine uncomfortably close to his ear and another thud into the desk in front of him. He dropped from the chair at the same time as Frank dived for the cover of the desk beside him.

'Two of them,' whispered Frank as he drew his Colt and sent two bullets screaming through the doorway.

Two more flashes cut into the blackness from the doorway but the bullets whistled harmlessly above the desk.

'They daren't show themselves,' whispered Frank. 'Send a couple of shots to keep them in the hall, then dive out of the right hand window, I'll take the left.'

Mark raised his gun above the top of the

desk and squeezed the trigger. Frank was already moving. Mark jumped to his feet, sent another bullet crashing into the hall, and leaped across the room. In one movement he dived into the window a fraction of a second after Frank's hand smashed into the window on his left. There was an ear shattering crash of glass as the two men left the study. As they hit the hard ground they tucked their heads onto their chests and rolled over in a quick somersault to leap to their feet and race towards their horses.

The noise of the shattering glass brought the two men in the hall tearing into the room and across to the broken windows. They raised their Colts and fired after the twisting black outlines which raced away to be lost in the darkness.

'No use chasin' them,' muttered Ed angrily as he turned away from the window.

'Wonder who they were?' mused Clay.

'Let's see what they were after,' said Ed striking a match and lighting the lamp.

'Good job we came in quiet an' spotted thet faint light under the door,' said Clay, 'otherwise we'd hev walked straight into bullets.'

The two men examined the room quickly. 'Looks like they've been through a few drawers,' observed Mason, 'but there's no tellin' if they took anythin'.'

'The lock on this drawer's been forced,' pointed out Duncan. 'There's a few coins scattered in the bottom. Maybe some cash has gone.'

'Could be a couple of no good thieves,' said Mason scratching his chin. 'Come on let's see if there's anything Warren wants.'

The two men settled down to search the house.

Dan hurried from the Ace of Spades shocked by the news that Frank and Mark were riding into the guns of Mason and Duncan. He swung into the saddle and rode towards the edge of town. He left his horse some distance from Clements' house and crept stealthily forward. He approached it from the side but was still a hundred yards from the house when the quietness of the night was shattered by the roar of Colts. Dan stiffened. The silence which followed seemed unending until split once again by more shots, followed by the shattering of glass. Dan saw two figures leap from the ground close to the house and run towards some trees. The darkness was split by the flash of Colts from the house, but Dan saw the figures merge into the darkness under the trees and a moment later the pound of hoofs heralded the escape of his brother and Mark.

The urge to follow Frank to Silas Linden's to see if he was all right was strong, but Dan realised he must get back to the Ace of Spades at once.

He was soon striding into the saloon and saw that Silas was still standing at the bar. Dan strolled across to the counter and as he sipped a beer he whispered to Silas.

'Warren been out?'

'No,' replied Silas. 'He hasn't missed you. Everything all right?'

'Frank an' Mark got away after a gun fight,' said Dan, 'expect they're all right. Don't know whether they were recognised, but we'll know as soon as Mason an' Duncan get back.'

Half an hour passed and Dan was leaning with his back to the counter studying the occupants of the saloon when Jake Warren came from the direction of his office. He walked up to Dan.

'What's keepin' Duncan and Mason?' he snapped impatiently and called for a whisky.

'Nothin',' smiled Dan nodding towards the door which opened to admit the two men.

They hurried across to Warren and held out a bundle of papers. He took them with a smile.

'Good work,' he praised.

'We disturbed a couple of cowpokes,' reported Mason.

'What! Any idea who they were?' asked Warren disturbed by the announcement.

Dan's hand drifted towards his Colt as he anxiously awaited the reply.

Duncan shook his head. 'Nope, it was too dark to see. Some money appeared to have gone. Reckon they were a couple of no good saddle tramps.'

Dan relaxed when he heard this relieving news.

'I'm for the Diamond D to study these,' said Warren, indicating the bundle of papers. 'Have your drinks on the house.'

'We'll stay in town to carry out our duty as sheriffs,' laughed Mason.

Warren grinned. 'Reckon you'd better.'

'I'll ride with you,' said Dan pushing himself from the bar.

'No need if you want a night in town,' replied Warren.

'The Lazy A may be around,' pointed out Dan. 'I'll ride with you.'

The two men left the Ace of Spades and

were soon riding out of Santa Rosa at a steady trot. The ride to the Diamond D was uneventful and Dan's attempts to glean information were unsuccessful.

The rancher bade Dan goodnight and Dan led the two horses to the stables. After unsaddling the animals and rubbing them down Dan made his way past the back of the buildings towards the bunkhouse. A light shone from a large window at the back of the ranchhouse and hearing voices Dan realised that although the curtains were drawn the window was open.

He glanced anxiously around and seeing no one about, he crept silently towards the house. He flattened himself against the wall and inched his way carefully nearer the window.

'Are all the documents there?' Dan recognised Gloria Linden's voice.

'Most of them I think,' replied Warren. 'With these in my possession it won't be a hard job to transfer them to my name an' then I'll own most of Santa Rosa. The deeds to some property which Clements held are not here and there may be some property I know nothing about.'

'What are you going to do about those?' asked Gloria.

'I believe they may be somewhere in the Ace of Spades,' replied Warren. 'I'm shore Clements had a safe there but it must be hidden somewhere.'

'Then that will only leave the Lazy A,' laughed Gloria.

'Shore, honey,' said Warren, 'an' it won't be long before we have thet; Mason, Duncan, an' Ferguson hev started work on thet to-night.'

'What happened?' asked Gloria.

'Stampeded some horses,' laughcd Warren. 'Jest a gentle reminder of what I threatened to do.'

'Be careful Jake,' concern showed in Gloria's voice. 'I want comfort and security that comes with money, you've got the money, Jake and...'

'You're what I want,' finished Warren.

'I can only just remember what home was like before mother died,' said Gloria. 'Ever since then my father's been a drunkard, look at the house and the ranch now, my life spoiled until I saw that you could give me back those things which had been lost. I don't want to lose them again, so be careful.'

'I'll be all right,' laughed Warren. 'What are you worried about?'

'Are you sure of Dan Ferguson?' asked Gloria.

Dan stiffened.

'Ferguson?' said Warren amazed that Gloria should doubt him. 'He saved my life to-night, beat the Lazy A foreman to the draw.' Gloria did not reply. 'Why are you suspicious of him?'

Gloria's voice was low when she answered and Dan moved nearer to the window, straining his ears to catch her reply.

'I was going to see my father to-day,' she said, 'thought he might know who really owns the Lazy A; but when I was still some distance from the house I saw someone go over to the stables. I could swear it was Mark Stevens!'

'What!' Warren gasped with surprise. 'But Ferguson killed him.'

'That's what I thought,' replied Gloria. 'Mind you, I was a good way from the house and I could have been mistaken.'

'Did you call on your father?' asked Warren.

'No, I went no further,' said Gloria. 'Thought I might scare whoever it was away and if it was Mark Stevens, I thought you'd better investigate.'

A chair scraped the floor and Dan heard

Warren pacing up and down the room.

'Another thing,' went on Gloria. 'I was in Merchant's Store and Doc Wilson was there. Amongst the things he had bought were some ladies hair combs.'

'Wal, what's thet got to do with it?' snapped Warren.

'If Stevens is alive then most likely Abigail Clements is too. Doc Wilson was in the Flats, could he have brought Abbe Clements out and back to his house?'

Warren stopped pacing up and down. Suddenly, he started to laugh. 'What you say is possible,' he agreed, 'but hardly likely. I think you've been letting your imagination run away with you. Look at it this way. Frank McCoy an' Mark Stevens daren't show up as near town as Silas's. Abbe couldn't hide at the Docs. It would be too risky with all the callers he gets, besides, we were there and saw no signs of her. You know the Doc often does some shopping for outlying ranchers; those combs could hev been for one of their wives.'

'I guess you're right,' replied Gloria. 'But all the same I'm worried, I could swear that was Mark Stevens.'

'If it will set your mind at rest,' said Warren gently, 'I'll visit both places in the morning, there are other things to think of to-night with you around.'

Realising that he would learn no more Dan slipped silently away from the window and made his way quickly to the bunkhouse where, knowing that he dare not leave the ranch for a while, he made a pretence of going to sleep.

An hour went by before Dan moved and making sure the other occupants of the bunkhouse were asleep, he dressed quickly and crept silently outside. He paused, allowing his eyes to become accustomed to the night. All was silent around the ranchhouse and he moved quietly to the stable where he quickly saddled a horse which he led for some distance before climbing into the saddle. He continued at a walking pace for a while before putting the animal into a fast trot towards Santa Rosa.

He slowed to a walk when he reached town and moved slowly along Main Street which was quiet in the early hours of the morning. Half way along the street Dan moved into the deep shadows on the opposite side of the street to the doctor's, halted his horse, and slipped from the saddle. He tied the animal to the hitching rail and drawing his Colt crept along stealthily. A block away from the doctor's he turned into a side alley and moving round the buildings came back along a narrow street almost opposite to the doctor's. He moved slowly and quietly towards the main street and was thankful for his precaution when he saw the glow of a cigarette in the darkness at the end of the street; Warren must not know he had visited Doc Wilson. He crept silently to within a few yards of the man when his foot caught a loose piece of wood. The man spun round but before he realised what was happening Dan leaped forward and brought down the barrel of his Colt on to the man's head with a hard bone breaking crash. The man sank to the ground without a groan.

Dan stepped over the body to survey the main street. All was silent and Dan quickly recovered his horse and hurried to Doc Wilson's. He tied his horse to the fence and seeing no one about he hurried up the path. He examined the windows and was thankful when he found one, the latch of which had not been placed fully home. With gentle persuasion he was able to force back the latch and open the window. He stepped quickly over the low sill and after closing the window behind him he found his way into the hall. He trod quietly up the stairs and knocked gently at the first door he came to. There was no immediate answer but when he tapped again, he saw the faint light under the door brighten and heard someone moving towards the door.

The door opened slowly. Dan stepped forward stifling the cry of amazement which sprang to Abbe's lips.

'It's all right,' whispered Dan reassuringly as he pushed Abbe gently back into the room. 'I'm Frank's brother.'

He felt the tension go out of the girl's body, and saw relief come into her eyes. He released his hold on her and continued his explanation.

'Sorry to come in on you this way,' he apologised, 'but I thought any knockin' might wake the neighbourhood and I didn't want to be seen.'

Abbe closed the door. 'Does Frank know you're here?' she asked.

'Yes,' replied Dan. 'He explained everything to me and I'm workin' with Warren.' He smiled when he saw the look of astonishment on Abbe's face. 'I overheard somethin' to-night and it's important thet you leave here.'

The note of urgency in Dan's tone convinced Abbe and she led the way to the other bedroom and Dan soon put them both in possession of the facts.

Doc Wilson agreed that Abbe should leave at once and preparations were soon made after he reassured her that he would be all right.

Dan and Abbe slipped quietly away from Santa Rosa and once on the trail to Fort Sumner put their mounts into a fast trot. Reaching the fork they left the trail and were soon pulling their horses to a halt outside Silas Linden's broken-down house. They climbed from the saddles and Dan hurried to the door to hammer loudly.

'All right, all right, I'm comin'.' They heard Silas muttering as he shuffled to the door.

He swung it back holding a lamp high. 'What on earth...' He stopped as the beam fell on Dan and Abbe. He gasped in amazement. 'Wal, I'll be blowed,' he said. 'Come inside quick. What's happened?'

Frank and Mark gasped with surprise when Abbe and Dan entered the ranch-house. Frank leaped to Abbe's outstretched arms.

'Are you all right?' he asked and when she nodded he turned to Dan. 'What's happened?'

Dan told his story over a cup of coffee. 'I figure thet the three of you could move into Abbe's house,' he concluded. 'Warren's had the place searched as you two well know,' he added with a grin. 'By the way, did you find anything?'

'Yes,' answered Frank producing a bundle of documents. 'Mark grabbed these when we were interrupted.'

'Any value?' asked Dan.

'Yes,' replied Frank. 'They are the deeds to a lot of property. There's also a letter for you, Abbe,' he said, handing her a long white envelope.

She looked at the front. 'Daddy's writing,' she whispered. She picked up a knife and quickly slit the envelope open. She drew out a sheet of notepaper and after a quick glance started to read. 'Dear Abbe, Should anything ever happen to me you will find an important letter and documents in a safe in the Ace of Spades. I had it specially made and hidden in my office. How you act after reading them is up to you. You will see how I have acted and if you will take the advice of your father, you will do exactly what I did – nothing; but it is nice to know it's there, in case. All my love, Dad. P.S. – If ever you try to move the furniture after I've gone don't do it on your own, it's very heavy.'

Everyone stared in silence at each other when she finished.

'What's it all about?' asked Mark.

'Any ideas, Abbe?' asked Dan.

The girl shook her head. 'I've no idea what Dad could be referring to,' she said.

'There's only one thing to do an' thet's to git thet letter,' pointed out Silas.

'Agreed,' said Frank, 'but thet's not goin' to be easy. There's nearly always someone about at the Ace of Spades an' we need time for someone to search for the safe.'

Plans were made, and half an hour later Silas listened to the fading hoof-beats as his friends rode away.

Chapter Fourteen

'Wal, Gloria, it's time to put your mind at rest,' said Jake Warren as he lit a cheroot after breakfast. 'I'll get Ferguson, pick up Duncan and Mason in town an' pay a visit to Doc Wilson an' your father. Meet me in the Ace of Spades this afternoon.'

He kissed her full on the lips and hurried from the house.

'Get me Ferguson,' he called to one of his cowboys as he walked to the stable where he was saddling a horse when the man returned.

'Ferguson rode out over an hour ago,' he said. 'Left a message to tell you he had a plan to hit the Lazy A hard and was ridin' to get Duncan and Mason.'

'Thet seems to prove Ferguson's on the level,' Warren muttered to himself. He paused leaning on the saddle thoughtfully. 'Still, there's no harm in checkin'.' He turned to the cowboy. 'Get three men and come with me.'

When they reached Santa Rosa they pulled

up outside the sheriff's office but finding no one there they headed for Doc Wilson's. Warren halted about a hundred yards from the doctor's and slipped from the saddle.

'We must take the doc by surprise. If anyone is with him we don't want to give them time to hide,' said Warren as the cowboys gathered round him. 'Cal, go an' check with Rody, he'll be in the alley opposite Wilson's.'

The cowboy hurried away and in a few moments came running back.

'Rody's dead,' he panted. 'His head split open.'

'What!' gasped Warren. He stared incredulously at the cowboy. 'Two of you see to him,' he snapped and hurried along the road followed by the other two men.

Reaching Doc Wilson's he flung open the gate, hurried up the path and crashed open the front door. The doctor who was coming down the stairs, stared in amazement as the door banged open.

Anger flared in his face when he saw Warren. 'What's the meaning of this?' he shouted.

Warren crossed the hall in three strides and grasped the doctor by his coat lapels. Fire smouldered in his eyes.

'I put two men to watch you,' he snarled.

'One was knocked out and robbed the other day. We've just found the other one dead. What do you know about it?'

The doctor stared wide-eyed at the rancher. 'Nothing. What should I know?'

Warren pushed the old man away in disgust. 'Where's Abbe Clements?' he snapped.

'We've been through all this before,' said the doctor wearily, fingering the bruises on his face. 'I've not seen her since the day her father was killed.'

'Search the house,' ordered Warren turning to his cowboys.

The men hurried away but in ten minutes they were both back to report that there was no sign of anyone else having been in the house.

'What made you think she was here?' smiled Wilson.

'You bought some ladies' hair-combs,' replied Warren.

The doctor laughed. 'Can't I shop for some of my patients?' he said.

Warren's eyes narrowed. 'If I find you've been holdin' out on me I'll kill you.' Warren swung on his heels and hurried from the house.

Finding Silas out when they reached the old ranch Warren's men searched the place thoroughly but found no trace of anyone other than Silas using the house. Warren swung into the saddle feeling he had wasted his time when one of his men interrupted his thoughts.

'How many horses has old Linden?' he asked.

'One,' replied Warren. 'Why?'

The cowboy looked thoughtful. 'Seems to me thet about three horses hev used the stable recently.'

Warren stared at the man. 'Then Gloria did see someone,' he whispered. 'But thet's no proof it was Mark Stevens. We'll check Ferguson when he gets back.' He looked at his men. 'Anyone check Doc Wilson's stable?'

The men shook their heads.

'Check it Cal,' ordered Warren. 'An' then report to the Ace of Spades.'

Cal nodded and the three men kicked their horses into a steady gallop towards Santa Rosa.

Dan kept his horse to a fast pace to Santa Rosa and found the town taking on the work of a new day when he pulled to a halt outside the sheriff's office. He greeted the two gun-men cordially as he walked into the office.

'What bring's you in?' asked Ed. 'Thought you hed to protect Warren.'

'He wants us to hit the Lazy A this morning; fire the buildings he said,' answered Dan.

'But thet would be easier an' better at night,' protested Duncan.

'Warren figures there won't be many cowpokes about,' replied Dan, 'what with the herds to look after an' those horses we set loose last night; besides he said it must be done this morning to fit in with a big scheme he has in mind.

'Guess we'd better ride,' said Mason.

The three men left the office and were soon in the saddles heading for the Lazy A. They pulled to a halt on the hill behind the ranchhouse and crept Indian fashion to the top to survey the buildings.

'No sign of life,' pointed out Duncan.

'Guess Warren figured correctly,' grunted Mason.

'Reckon it might be better to leave the horses where they are,' said Dan. 'It'll be easier to slip down unseen if there is anyone about.'

They agreed on their plan of campaign and slipped over the skyline to creep quickly but silently down the hillside. They reached the back of the bunkhouse and still there was no sign of anyone.

'This is dead easy,' grinned Mason. 'Now fer one big fire.'

'Hold it!' a voice rapped from the ranch-house.

The three men spun round to see a cow-boy step from the back door of the house. Mason and Duncan gasped, staring at the man as if they had seen a ghost. A tin star was pinned to a brown shirt.

'McCoy!' hissed Mason. 'But I thought...' he glanced sharply at Dan. His body tensed and his hand flew with the speed of a snake to his Colt.

Dan spun sideways and crashed his fist into Mason's face, sending him crashing to the ground, to find himself staring into the muzzle of Dan's gun. As Dan crossed in front of him Duncan jerked his Colt from its holster but before he could squeeze the trigger it was sent spinning from his grasp by Frank's accurate shot.

'Good work, Frank,' complimented Dan as his brother walked up.

The two gunmen glared at Dan. 'Sold us out,' snapped Mason. 'Warren'll get you for this.'

'We'll see what Warren has to say when he

meets three people from the graves above the Alamogordo,' smiled Dan as Mark and Abbe leading the horses appeared from behind the ranch house.

The two gunmen stared incredulously.

'Then you've been in with them all the time,' snarled Duncan.

'Shore,' grinned Dan. 'Funny part is thet on our way to the Diamond D last night Warren told me all about how you killed Clements, so he seized the opportunity to frame my brother.'

'It's a lie,' yelled Mason. 'It was Warren's idea to kill Clements – he hired us to do it – so that he could frame the sheriff an' get him out of the way; he didn't think of it afterwards.'

Dan grinned. 'Thanks fer the confession, Mason, mine was only a good guess, but I reckoned it would be near the mark. Now let's get goin'.'

Silas Linden was riding at a steady pace towards Santa Rosa when he heard the sound of hard ridden horses approaching a bend in the trail. He pulled his horse sharply off the trail to the cover of some huge boulders and held it steady as the hoof-beats grew louder. Three horsemen pounded past.

'Warren!' whispered Silas to himself. 'This gives me a great chance.'

As soon as the horsemen had disappeared in a swirl of dust Silas climbed into the saddle and put his horse into a fast gallop towards town. He slackened his pace when he reached the main street and rode slowly to the Ace of Spades. He hitched his horse to the rail and strolled casually along the sidewalk until he reached the alley which ran along the side of the saloon. He glanced up and down the street and seeing that he was attracting no attention he stepped quickly into the alley. When he reached the window, which he knew was in Warren's office, he tested it but found it locked. Pulling a large handkerchief from his pocket he wrapped it round his fist and drove it sharply against the glass close to the catch.

Silas looked round nervously licking his dry lips, but the sound of shattering glass disturbed no one. He reached inside, unfastened the catch, raised the window, and climbed into the room. He paused a moment surveying the room, bearing in mind the letter which Abbe had received. The postscript in the letter had intrigued Silas and he felt it must have something to do with the hidden safe.

A large desk occupied a position at one end of the room, a little way off the wall. Along one wall there was a long sideboard while on another there was a large bookcase. Silas figured that these three pieces must be the heavy furniture referred to by Clements and as he eyed them he thought that the obvious place for a safe to be hidden would be in the wall behind either the sideboard or the bookcase. Time was precious to Silas so he took the easiest first, but found no sign of a safe behind the sideboard. The bookcase was a more formidable piece to move but Silas worked quickly and methodically, and by the time he was able to move the bookcase, half the books had been removed and sweat poured from the grey haired man. He strained at the bookcase and gradually moved one end from the wall until he had sufficient room to squeeze behind it. He searched the wall methodically, but without success. Wearily, the disappointed man sat down in the chair behind the desk. He mopped his brow wondering where the safe could be. The only piece of furniture left was the desk and that wasn't covering any part of a wall. Silas stared at the highly polished mahogany. Suddenly, he sat upright.

'The floor! Of course the floor!' he whispered to himself. 'No one would ever dream of putting a safe in the floor, but wasn't that exactly what Clements wanted, a place no one would think about.'

Silas was on his feet pushing at the heavy desk. Slowly it moved forward as he strained with all his strength. A shout of triumph escaped from his lips as one of the ends revealed a safe beneath it. Quickly, Silas was on his knees inserting the key which he found in a box let into the floor underneath the other leg of the desk. Eagerly he swung open the door of the safe and reached inside.

'Thank you Silas I'll take care of that.' The cold even toned voice startled Silas. He looked up wide-eyed to find himself staring into the muzzle of a Colt held in Jake Warren's right hand. His left hand was extended towards Silas to receive the large envelope which Silas had removed from the safe.

Slowly Silas rose to his feet cursing himself for being so careless. In his excitement his ears had closed to all sounds. He handed the envelope to Warren who coldly smiled his thanks.

'It is very good of you to find this for me,' he said smoothly. 'It must be very valuable to be hidden in such a good hiding place.'

Warren's tone changed, his eyes narrowed. 'Over by the wall,' he snarled, motioning with his gun. 'Face it an' if you so much as move this gun will blast daylight into you.'

Silas glared at Warren and shuffled slowly to the wall. When he heard the rancher tearing at the envelope he was tempted to turn and rush him, but he knew it would be useless. He heard Warren chuckle to himself as he read the contents of the envelope.

A sharp tap at the door interrupted Warren's chuckle as he studied the papers.

'Come in,' he shouted.

The door opened and Cal escorted Doc Wilson into the room at the point of his Colt. The doctor hesitated in his step when he saw Silas, hands raised above his head, standing against the wall. Warren smiled at Wilson's astonishment.

'Come right in, doc,' he said. 'Jest caught this old man taking, or rather discovering some important documents. What did you find out, Cal?'

'There's been more than one horse in Doc Wilson's stable recently, thought I'd better bring him along,' replied Cal.

'Hear that, Silas,' called Warren. 'We found the same evidence at your place an' Gloria said she thought she saw Mark Stevens there; an' how did you know about this safe if you haven't been in touch with Miss Clements?'

Silas remained silent and after a brief pause Warren nodded to Cal. The cowboy grabbed Silas by the shoulder and pulled him round sharply, driving his fist into the old man's face. Silas slumped back against the wall; Cal hit him hard in his mouth and as Silas slid to the floor blood flowed from the gashes.

'Talk, Silas, talk!' yelled Warren as he stood over the crumpled form.

Cal dragged Silas up against the wall and drove two hard blows into his stomach. The old man doubled up, but as he fell forward Cal's fist crashed across his right eye, opening a huge slit across the eyebrow. Silas fell to the floor.

'Where's Abbe Clements?' shouted Warren. Silas shook his head. 'Talk, you stupid old fool. Can't you see I've the upper hand?'

Silas spat blood from his cut mouth. 'Dan will get you,' he croaked.

Cal stepped forward menacingly, but Warren stopped him.

'Ferguson will be in fer a nice surprise when he gets back,' laughed Warren. His eyes narrowed as he swung round on the doctor. 'You goin' to talk or hev the same treatment.'

Doc Wilson did not speak and Warren nodded to Cal who stepped towards the doctor. He slapped the back of his hand hard across Wilson's face jerking his head sideways. Cal drew his arm back preparing another blow when he was halted by a tap on the door. He looked sharply at Warren, but before the rancher could speak the door opened. Warren grinned when he saw Mason and Duncan enter the room.

'Come right in,' he called. 'We've got all...' His voice faded and the smile vanished when he saw Dan and Frank, Colts in hands, follow the two gunmen into the room. He stared unbelievingly when Mark Stevens and Abbe Clements walked in and closed the door.

'Mister Linden!' gasped Abbe when she saw Silas's battered face. She rushed across the room to him.

'Ferguson,' snarled Warren, 'you double...'

Dan smiled. 'Not Ferguson, please! McCoy,' he interrupted quietly.

'McCoy?' Warren gasped.

'Frank's brother,' replied Dan curtly.

Warren stared wide-eyed at Dan and moved from behind the desk.

'I figured you'd framed Frank,' continued Dan coldly. 'These two hired guns have confessed so it's all up, Warren, your bid for power has finished.' He walked over to Silas. 'You all right, Silas?' he asked.

Silas nodded. 'The documents I found in the safe in the floor are on the desk.'

Dan picked up the envelope. 'Abbe, you should open this, it is addressed to you.'

Abbe took the envelope and pulled out the papers. She looked at them quickly and then read the letter. 'Dear Abbe. You will see from the documents in this envelope that the Lazy A spread belongs to you. I have kept it a secret not wanting the townsfolk to think I was a grabbing man. You will also see that I have discovered gold on the ranch.'

'Gold!' everyone gasped, interrupting Abbe who stared incredulously at the paper.

Dan stared at Warren. 'You knew about the gold, thets why you wanted Clements out of the way and of course Frank and Abbe who also stood in your way.'

'Not quite right, McCoy,' said Warren. 'I'm cornered so I may as well admit thet I knew about the gold but I didn't know thet Clements owned the Lazy A until I saw those documents. Clements stood in my way because of the property he owned in town and the influence he had.'

'But why didn't your father use the gold?' asked Frank, staring at Abbe.

Abbe who had continued reading the letter explained. 'He says he did not want Santa Rosa spoiling by a gold rush. He didn't need the money and hopes I shan't have to throw the place open to the gold diggers.'

A tap at the door interrupted Abbe and before anyone could reach the door it opened and Gloria Linden stepped inside. She stared round the room in amazement and was startled when she saw her father's bruised and battered face.

'Dad!' she cried. The love which had been deep inside her all these years burst to the surface as she flew across the room towards him.

Warren seized the opportunity so unexpectedly offered to him. As Gloria passed in front of him he grabbed her arm and pulled her close to him as a shield. At the same time, he pulled a small gun from a shoulder holster.

'Drop your guns,' he snarled, 'or else Gloria gets it.'

Dan and Frank dropped their Colts instantly, realising that Warren now held the upper hand. Duncan, Mason and Cal grinned and were about to step forward when Silas with tremendous effort leaped from his chair and flung himself at Warren.

'Leave my girl alone!' he yelled, but the words died on his lips as Warren's gun spat bullets to halt him in his rush. He jerked to a stop, his hands grasping his stomach and he sank slowly to the floor.

As Warren fired Gloria grasped his wrist and seeing her father hit she struggled like some wild animal trying to free itself.

Mark's Colt was already in his hand covering the hired guns. Doc Wilson rushed to Silas but realised there was nothing he could do. Dan leaped forward towards Warren, but stopped in his tracks as another shot rocked the room. A look of disbelief crossed Warren's face, his grip on Gloria relaxed, and he slumped to the floor, a dark red stain slowly marking his shirt across his chest, the gun still in his hand. Gloria stared in horror at the body for a brief moment and then was on her knees beside her father.

'Dad, dad, are you all right?' she cried, her voice full of tenderness.

A faint smile flicked across his face. 'Dear Gloria, it's wonderful to hear you speak like that again. I can die happy now.'

'Oh! No!' Gloria sobbed. 'I need you.'

'You'll be all right,' assured Silas. 'Frank here promised to set up the ranch again if I helped him. I'm sure he'll pay that debt to you.'

'Of course, I will Silas,' said Frank. 'Your ranch borders Abbe's so we'll see Gloria's all right.'

'If Frank is giving up as sheriff then I'll be on the look out for a job as well,' said Mark. 'Maybe Gloria will give me a job as foreman?'

'A good idea, son,' smiled Silas as he saw Mark take Gloria's hand comfortingly in his. 'You're ... all ... so kind.'

The publishers hope that this book has given you enjoyable reading. Large Print Books are especially designed to be as easy to see and hold as possible. If you wish a complete list of our books please ask at your local library or write directly to:

Dales Large Print Books
Magna House, Long Preston,
Skipton, North Yorkshire.
BD23 4ND

This Large Print Book, for people
who cannot read normal print,
is published under the auspices of

THE ULVERSCROFT FOUNDATION